Uncle Max used to sit me on his shoulders when I was small. It was like being on top of a huge tree. Uncle Max's strong brown arms were the branches, ready to catch me if I fell off. Once, I remember that I cried and cried for Uncle Max to take me on his shoulders to the park to see if I was taller than the slides. He said he couldn't.

"But Daddy takes me," I protested.

"One day, little Lily, one day. When we have freedom, you and I will go to the park."

His voice was so grave that I calmed down, but I still didn't understand that Uncle Max wasn't allowed to take me—a little white girl—to the park because he was black. When the police took Daddy away, I didn't understand that as well.

Other Books by Beverley Naidoo

JOURNEY TO JO'BURG

CHAIN OF FIRE

NO TURNING BACK

THE OTHER SIDE OF TRUTH

WEB OF LIES

OUT OF BOUNDS

Seven Stories of Conflict and Hope

Beverley Naidoo

📖 HarperTrophy®

An Imprint of HarperCollins*Publishers*

Out of Bounds: Seven Stories of Conflict and Hope
Copyright © 2001 by Beverley Naidoo

"The Dare" was previously published as "Poinsettias" in
Global Tales by Longman, © 1997 by Beverley Naidoo

"The Typewriter" was first published in
Knockout Short Stories by Longman, © 1998 by Beverley Naidoo

"The Gun" was first published in
That'll Be the Day by Bell & Hyman, © 1998 by Beverley Naidoo

"The Playground" was first published in
Just in Time by Puffin, © 1999 by Beverley Naidoo

"The Noose," "One Day, Lily, One Day," and "Out of Bounds"
© 2001 by Beverley Naidoo

Library of Congress Cataloging-in-Publication Data
Naidoo, Beverley
   Out of Bounds : seven stories of conflict and hope / by Beverley Naidoo
      p.   cm.
   Summary: Seven stories, spanning the time period from 1948 to 2000, chron-
icle the experiences of young people from different races and ethnic groups as they
try to cope with the restrictions placed on their lives by South Africa's apartheid
laws.
   ISBN 978-0-06-050801-2 (pbk.)
   1. Apartheid—Juvenile fiction. 2. Children's stories, South African (English)
[1. Apartheid—Fiction. 2. Race relations—Fiction. 3. South Africa—Fiction.
4. Short stories.] I. Title.
PZ7.N1384Ou 2003   2002068901
[Fic]—dc21   CIP
                                                                     AC

Typography by Hilary Zarycky
❖
First Harper Trophy edition, 2008
First U.S. Edition, 2003
Originally published in 2001 by Puffin Books, a division of the Penguin Group,
London, England

For Nandha

CONTENTS

FOREWORD

When apartheid came to an end, the world had expected South Africa to be overwhelmed by the bloodbath of a race war. This did not happen. Instead the world watched with wonder and awe as South Africans of all races participated in the first democratic elections of 1994. Many had believed that once a black-led government was in power, South Africa would be devastated by an orgy of revenge and retribution. Instead of revenge and retribution the world marveled as those who had been made to suffer so much and so needlessly as the victims of the vicious policy of apartheid, revealed a remarkable magnanimity and generosity of spirit in their willingness to forgive their tormentors and oppressors—a spirit embodied spectacularly in the person of Nelson Mandela.

Reading Beverley Naidoo's short stories, I realize with some shock just how utterly reasonable were those dire expectations about what was in store for our beloved country. Apartheid inflicted untold and unnecessary suffering on people just because of their skin color. They were demeaned and humiliated in a manner that is now difficult to imagine when almost no one in present-day South Africa admits that they ever supported such a vicious policy. Those who were ill-treated in this fashion should, by rights, have been filled with resentment and bitterness and should have wanted to settle scores by getting their own back.

Yes, it is amazing that they have, by and large, not done so. I was surprised by the intensity of my feelings as I read these stories, carefully crafted with such consummate skill and with such deft touches. The stories are taut and the tension and suspense become quite unbearable. Alfred Hitchcock would have been in his element. I was often a little scared to get to the denouement for I was uncertain of the outcome.

Most of what is described here no longer happens in the new South Africa. But this record is important so that we South Africans can never with any degree of credibility deny that we could reach such depths of depravity. There is a beast in each of us, and none of us can ever say we would never be guilty of such evil. We must acknowledge that it happened. But most importantly we should, after reading these quite disturbing stories, renew our commitment to the new democracy and its new culture of respect for fundamental human rights and say for ourselves and our descendants, "Never again will we want to treat fellow human beings in this fashion."

And I hope and pray that others in other lands may commit themselves to ensure that such evil will never be tolerated and that they will not be guilty of perpetrating it.

ARCHBISHOP DESMOND MPILO TUTU

September 2000

INTRODUCTION

The struggle for justice within South Africa was, for many years, a symbol across the world. But at the end of the twentieth century, history was turned upside down. The oppressors opened their prison doors and sat down with those they had oppressed . . . people they had locked behind bars for years or driven out of the country. They exchanged words instead of bullets. Was it possible, together, to make "a new South Africa"?

To understand a little of this enormous task, we need to look back in time. Europeans arrived 350 years ago at the Cape in great sailing ships. Some came looking for riches, some for adventure, some fleeing persecution because of their religion. They found a vast open land that was rich for farming and people who would have shared it with them. But the Europeans set themselves apart, putting up fences wherever they settled. They wanted the land only for themselves and used their guns to get it. They fought wars with many groups of Africans, slowly moving further inland and extending their boundaries. When they could not get enough Africans to work for them, they brought in people from Asia.

The Dutch were the first settlers. Then came the British. The descendants of the Dutch became known as the Afrikaners—or "Boers," meaning "farmers." At times, the Afrikaners and the English-speaking settlers fought each other, especially after the discovery of diamonds and gold. But most Europeans were agreed on one thing: there was a ladder in life and that "White" people should be at the top. Below came "Coloreds," a name given to people mainly of mixed European and African heritage. Then came Indians and, at the lowest rung, black Africans.

Some of the Afrikaners supported Hitler in the Second World War, and when they took over the government in 1948, they tightened the ladder of racism through hundreds of laws. Everyone had to be classified by their so-called race. The definitions were scientific nonsense, such as:

> A "White" person means a person who in appearance obviously is, or who is generally accepted as, a White person, but does not include a person who, although in appearance obviously a White person, is generally accepted as a Colored person.

This "goobledygook" became law, and the policy was called apartheid. In the Timeline Across Apartheid, you can read about some of its terrible laws. Hundreds of thousands of people who broke them were thrown into jail. In June 1976, black schoolchildren faced tanks and were shot. But, in the end, those in power could not control people's anger. On February 11, 1990, the world watched as Nelson Mandela, South Africa's most famous prisoner, walked out of jail to help negotiate a new future. Four years later, he became South Africa's first democratically elected President—the first black President and leader of a "rainbow government."

Each of these stories is set in a different decade during the last half of the twentieth century and into the twenty-first. My characters are caught up in a happening from that particular time. They inhabit a most beautiful land but one that has been full of barriers—real walls and those in the mind. Some people have accepted these, while others have challenged them. There have been many different tests for the human spirit in South Africa— the land in which I was born—and they are the stuff of my stories.

BEVERLEY NAIDOO

THE DARE

1948

Marika thrust the glass jar up to Veronica's face.

"See this one, Nicky!" she declared. "Caught it last week!" Veronica stared at the coiled brown shape slithering inside the greenish liquid. She felt sick.

"You should have seen how blinking quick I was, man! This sort are poisonous!"

Marika's eyes pinned her down, watching for a reaction. She didn't know which were worse, Marika's or those of the dead creature in the jar.

"Where did you find it?"

Her voice did not betray her, and Marika began her dramatic tale about tracking the snake in the bougainvillea next to the hen run.

It was a valuable addition to her collection. Rows of bottles, all with the same green liquid, lined the shelf above her bed. Spiders and insects of various shapes and sizes floated safely, serenely, inside. Marika carefully replaced the snake next to another prize item—a one-legged chameleon, its colors dulled and fixed. Veronica remembered it alive. It had been the farm children's pet briefly until they had tired of capturing flies for it. She had even helped one whole Saturday prowling around the cowshed, sneaking up and snapping the overfed blue buzzers in cigarette tins. The next morning Marika and her brothers had decided to let the creature go free and get its own dinner. But when they had come to release the catch of the splintering old wood-and-wire hutch, the chameleon lay stiff and still. The three boys had wanted to make a special grave down in the donga—but in the end Marika had persuaded them to let her preserve it.

The farm, a small holding owned by Marika's parents, lay against a mountain in the middle of the Magaliesberg. As well as growing fruit and vegetables and keeping a few animals, the van Reenens rented out a small cottage on the farm, mostly to city visitors. It was near enough to Johannesburg for Mr. and Mrs. Martin with their only child, Veronica, to get away from the ever-increasing hustle for short breaks. They were regulars, coming two or three times a year. In fact, Mr. Martin had been visiting since he was a child, when Marika's mother herself had been a small girl on the same farm. Veronica's own memories of the place stretched back for as long as she could remember. For years she and Marika had played "house" in the donga behind the farmhouse. They had used larger stones for the walls, shifting around smaller stones as the furniture. In the past Veronica used to bring all her dolls, despite her mother's protests. Sensing Marika's envy, she had enjoyed saying which dolls could be played with. But since Marika's tenth birthday things were different.

Veronica had been taken by surprise. She had been sitting with the farm children on the wall of the stoep, dangling her legs and kicking the brickwork with her heels like the others. Marika had been telling her about her birthday treat when Veronica had suggested that they go to the donga.

"Hey, the girls are going to play dollies!" Marika's twin brother, Piet, had sneered. Slipping off the wall, six-year-old Dirk had rolled on the ground, kicking his legs in the air and cooing.

"Gaga gaga! Mommy! Mommy! Change my nappy!"

Veronica had glared at him, and he had pulled a face at her. She had fought to hold back her tears. Only Anton, the oldest, had not joined in but called the others to leave the girls alone to their sissy games. Marika had reacted furiously.

"I'm not a sissy!" she had screamed after them. Leaving Veronica alone on the stoep, she had gone inside the house, slamming the door behind her.

When Veronica returned to the farm a few months later, Marika had begun her bottle collection. Veronica had also left her dolls at home, except for the eyelid-clicking, brown-eyed Margaret. But this time the porcelain head with brown painted curls remained tucked under the bedclothes and was spoken to only at night. She became Veronica's personal counselor on the farm—a pale replica of Veronica's personal counselor in town.

Back home in Johannesburg it was Rebecca, their maid, to whom Veronica confided. She was a far better listener than Margaret because she made sympathetic noises. With Veronica's mother often helping out at her father's office, or busy with Mothers' Union meetings, they spent a lot of time together. Whether she was cooking, washing, ironing, or dusting, Rebecca was always prepared to chat. But she never came to the farm with them. Instead she went to visit her own children, living with their grandmother, a five-hour bus ride away.

Sharing secrets with Rebecca was fun, especially when Rebecca had let her visit her dim, tiny room in the servants' quarters at the top of their block of flats. It had started with her desperate desire to see the bedspread that Rebecca had been patiently embroidering for months on "baby-sitting" nights when Veronica's parents went out. Although Veronica didn't think she needed to be "baby-sat," she liked Rebecca's company. Together they would sit and talk at the table in the Martins's kitchen until it was her bedtime. She had watched the bed-spread growing and, when it was finally com-pleted, had begged and nagged to see how it looked on the bed. But before she could be taken, Rebecca had made her promise, "Remember, you are not to tell your ma or pa!"

Because it had been a secret, everything had stayed fixed in her mind like a picture. The splen-did bedcover draped over an old iron bed raised up high on bricks. A curtain across one corner of the room, Rebecca's cupboard. An orange-crate table next to the bed, on which stood a photo of

Rebecca's four children. Veronica had studied their smiling black faces to see if they looked like their mother, trying to match the faces to the names she asked Rebecca to repeat. The only one whose name she always remembered was Selo, the oldest, because he was exactly her age and his name was shorter than the others.

"Is this Selo?" she had asked, picking out the tallest of the children, who had a cheerful, cheeky grin.

"Oh yes, that's Selo! Always getting into trouble!" Rebecca had laughed, adding, "But he's a good boy."

Yet here on the farm there was no Rebecca. So it was to Margaret that Veronica confided about the snake's awful eyes. Of course if it were Rebecca, she would make some sounds to show how disgusted she was. Then they would laugh together at how stupid it was to keep all those dead creatures in jars.

But there was something even more important she needed to talk to Rebecca about. It was something Marika had said after she had put the snake back on the shelf. She had hinted strongly that her brothers had made up a test that Veronica would have to pass before she could go on playing with them. Marika herself had carried out a dare set by the boys. She would not say what it had been, it was so terrible. She was equally mysterious about Veronica's dare.

"I'm not allowed to tell . . . but you know our neighbor Jan Venter . . . ?"

Marika had stopped and ominously refused to say anything more.

Big and burly—known for his flaming red beard, moustache, and temper—children, and even adults, usually kept clear of Meneer Venter when possible. Veronica had seen him only once, when he had come to see Mr. van Reenen to insist Marika's father mend the fence between them.

Jan Venter ran one of the biggest orange estates in the area, and everyone knew that he threatened to shoot any trespasser on his land like he shot baboons. That was not to be taken lightly. He was also known to be "fond of the bottle," and there had been talk about the disappearance of Mrs. Venter a few years ago. Some people said she had just had enough of his temper and gone back to her own people in another part of the country.

The rumor among the local children was that he had murdered his wife and buried her in front of his house—under a poinsettia bush that now had brighter-than-usual red flowers.

The next morning, instead of darting off early to look for Marika, Veronica hung back and waited for her parents before going to the farmhouse for breakfast. Marika and her family ate in the kitchen, but the Martins were served their meals in the dining room, beneath a pair of massive kudu horns and heavily framed photographs of Marika's grandparents. Mrs. van Reenen followed behind the servant who carried the plates of steaming porridge.

"Still no sign of rain, but it'll be a nice day again for you all!"

She smiled and stopped to pass on some of the local news, including talk of a leopard seen on the mountain behind the farm.

Today Veronica took her time. When she came to her last piece of toast, she chewed it slowly. She was trying to think of a good reason to stay with her parents, who were pouring second cups of coffee, when her mother said, "You can be excused, Veronica dear. You can go off and play.

You won't go near the mountain, will you?"

She nodded, pursing her lips together and got up. Her father ruffled her hair as she passed.

"Have a good day, Ronnie!"

He only called her that when he was relaxed. She just hoped Marika's brothers didn't ever hear it. Their jokes about "Nicky" were bad enough.

Hoping the van Reenen children might still be at breakfast in the kitchen, Veronica headed for the opposite door, to the stoep. But they were already there on the wall, legs swinging, waiting. Anton, the oldest, was direct.

"We've made a new rule. Girls have to do a dare before they join our gang."

Veronica stood rooted to the concrete floor. All the children except Anton were grinning. Deadpan, he went on to explain that she had to climb through the barbed-wire fence into the neighboring Venter estate and make her way across to the front of Jan Venter's farmhouse.

"You've got to get one of his poinsettia flowers. We don't have any this side, so you can't cheat!"

They would accompany her as far as the fence and wait for her to return.

There was no way out. If she wasn't part of the

gang, there would be no one to play with. As they marched across the donga Veronica glanced at the spot where they used to play "house" in the shade of the thorn trees. The stones were still there. It was like another world. Inside she felt cold and shivery even though her feet and arms were moving swiftly in step with the others and the sun's heat was already enveloping them. As they trudged in silence along the edge of the mealie field, nearing the wire fence, Dirk suddenly broke out into a jingle.

"Nicky, Nicky, looks so sicky!"

He was told sharply to shut up by the others.

"A dare is not a game! It's a serious thing, you idiot," Marika snapped.

At the fence Anton and Piet parted the barbed wire for Veronica to slip through. Anton pointed.

"The farmhouse is that way. At the end of the orange trees follow the road."

Veronica cast a quick glimpse back at the group. They all had solemn faces except for Dirk who couldn't hide his little grin. She was already far down the line of orange trees when she heard Marika's voice ringing faintly behind her.

"Good luck, hey, Nicky!"

Sounds of laughter seemed to follow.

For as far as she could see ahead there were only straight rows of trees, the deep green leaves and bright orange fruit silently glinting in the sunlight. They were not good cover. With her shadow darting from one tree's patch of shade to the next, her mind began searching wildly for what to say if she was caught. Could she pretend she was lost . . . or that she had a dog which had gotten lost? Or that she had come to warn Meneer Venter about the leopard on the mountain? Veronica could not imagine the big burly man with the flaming beard believing any of her stories. She almost wished the dare had been for her to go up the mountain instead.

Her mouth was dry, her body wet and sticky, her legs sprinting heavily. Sucking in small quick breaths, she jerked to a halt. What on earth was she doing here, alone in the middle of Jan Venter's oranges? This dare was too dangerous. She should run back and tell the others it was unfair. She bet they wouldn't do it! Then she remembered Marika saying her own dare was too terrible to talk about. Perhaps she had just said that to frighten her. . . . But if she went back now, that would be the end of their friendship. Whatever could she do by herself on the farm? It wasn't worth thinking about. Lips pressed together, her eyes intently scoured the bushes ahead.

At last she could see she was coming to a dirt road. Peering from behind a tree, she studied how to make her way up it. On either side was a line of tall gray blue gums leading to a cluster of white-washed buildings. The furthest one seemed to be the main house. There was no poinsettia in sight, so the front had to be around one of the other sides. Behind the blue gums on the far side of the road, set a little back, were some huts—servants' quarters. Usually she hardly took any notice of these kind of buildings. They were just there, part of what you found on a farm. But now she was forced to scan the area around the huts very closely. Although there were some open doorways, they were too dark to see inside. No one seemed to be around, either on the road or in the workers' compound, but it would be safer to stay on the side where she was for as long as possible. A few large avocado trees would provide thick cover for a short stretch—and then she would have to trust to the blue gums and to fortune.

At last, in line with the main house, she crossed the road. Her shoes smacking against the sand pounded as loudly as her heart. Facing her was a door, leading to a backyard. She ducked down to creep past a window. A few paces more and she had reached the side of the raised stoep. On tiptoe she stretched to look. Still no one! Through the wooden railings she glimpsed a spray of pointed red flowers. The poinsettia was just around the corner! Making a final dash to the bush, she ripped off a flower at the stem. Milky white stuff spurted out onto her fingers. Not bothering to wipe off the stickiness, she turned to run. But a door banging and fearsome shouting forced her to cower back next to the poinsettia bush and freeze.

"Jou bliksem! Ek sal jou moer!"

It could only be Jan Venter. Veronica's Afrikaans was not very good despite the lessons at school. But she knew Meneer Venter was swearing and that "moer" was probably "murder." Who was he going to murder now? Was she not perhaps already standing on his wife?

The commotion got worse. She could hear sounds of running and other people coming outside. An elderly woman in housemaid's uniform hurried down steps from the stoep close by to Veronica, without noticing her huddled against the wall. She was moaning softly to herself. Meneer Venter was shouting about people who stole from him. Everyone would see now what he did to thieves.

Veronica was trembling, but she had to find out what was happening. She stretched forward to see around the corner. A small number of servants stood at a short distance from the massive figure—his face just a shade lighter than his blazing beard and hair. In front of him stood a black child with thin spindly legs, wearing a pair of torn khaki shorts, his eyes fixed on the ground. The man grabbed the boy's ear and jerked his head upward, with his other hand forcing an orange into the boy's face.

"*Kyk hierso!* Look at this! I'll teach you a lesson you'll never forget!"

"Please, Baas, this boy has learnt his lesson. He won't do it again, Baas. I will speak to him, Baas!"

It was the old housemaid, her hands together as if in a prayer, pleading, moving nearer to Meneer Venter. His arm swept out, dismissing her.

"He must learn a proper lesson. Talking is not good enough!"

The old woman was insistent. "He's only a child, my Baas. Once the Baas was also a child!"

Meneer Venter turned on her now. "You go too far now, Lettie. Watch out or I'll give you a lesson too!"

The old woman covered her face with her hands, shaking her head.

Meneer Venter shouted instructions to a couple of servants who disappeared through the side door. One came back with a wooden chair and the other with a cane. For a moment after his ear had been released, the boy looked around wildly. In the second that Veronica glimpsed his eyes, she almost called out. He looked like Selo, Rebecca's son, in the photograph! It couldn't be him, could it? Rebecca's family lived far away. But Rebecca had said Selo was always getting into trouble.

The boy was ordered to lean over the chair. One of the male workers was ordered to stand in front and hold him down. Meneer Venter took the cane. Veronica did not look after the first two strikes. The boy's cries pierced her ears. She was shivering all over. Her stomach heaved.

When the cries reduced to a soft whimpering, Veronica looked up. To her horror Meneer Venter was walking in her direction in a slow swagger. There was no time and no where to run. Standing transfixed, she dropped the flower she was holding in her hand. His eyes were odd, glazed, as if not seeing anything. Then, as he drew close, they flickered.

"*Jy is 'n van Reenen, nè?* Tell your father I'm satisfied with the fence."

Before Veronica could even think what to say, he patted her hair lightly and walked on, up the steps and into the house. He had thought she was Marika.

Guiltily, Veronica looked down at the fallen poinsettia. She was aware of the old woman gently holding the boy, making soothing noises. The servants were talking quietly among themselves. Hastily she picked up the blood-red flower. The milky oozing had stopped and sealed up the stem. Grabbing a branch above her, she snapped off four more stems, careless of the sticky sap. A flower each. Sprinting down the road, she passed the old woman and the boy who had begun making their way painfully toward the huts behind the blue gums. No sounds followed as she entered the orange trees. She stopped running. She could walk the rest of the way now and give herself time to regain her breath. Then she could present each flower quite calmly. She might even take the gang some oranges.

THE NOOSE

1955

The year I turned ten, apartheid gripped me fully by the throat for the first time. Of course its fingers had been there all along, but I had been too busy to take much notice. In school I had to watch out for the tentacles of my slipper-happy teacher. At home, next door, it was Mrs. Busybody James. She was always lurking behind her net curtains and would tell Mommy everything and anything. When her little terrier, Wolfie, lunged at my ankles, I couldn't even give him a quick kick without her complaining. As soon as she saw Mommy turn the corner of the road, her flip-flops would be flapping down the polished red steps of her front stoep. Mommy could be struggling with a fat bundle of sewing in one arm and my little sister Lisa in the other, but Mrs. James wouldn't even wait for Mommy to reach our house and off-load before starting.

"Shame, Mrs. Peters, it's not nice to see a boy

mistreating a small creature like my Wolfie. . . ."

And that would be just the beginning. Funny but she never complained to Pa. She would just say "Good morning, Mr. Peters" or "Good evening, Mr. Peters" as if butter could melt in her mouth. I think she looked up to Pa because he was a supervisor in a clothing factory.

But my sharpest "red alert" was not switched on for Mrs. James nor my teacher. It was for when Omar, Billy, and I walked into town, ready for the white boys who tried to storm us whenever they caught us passing their patch. Their younger brothers and sisters had tangled hair, smudged faces, and running noses and played games on the pavements like the little children down our streets. They were even the same games. The boys with their marbles and beaten-up Dinky cars. The girls with their one-armed dolls and skipping ropes tied to drunk-looking fences or gates. Sometimes they shouted names after us, or even tried to throw stones, but usually we ignored the young ones. If we did anything back, some adult would always be in the house and that would mean a lot bigger trouble! Of course if the older boys trapped us, those adults were not going to help us. Once when

I managed to pin down my attacker, and Omar and Billy were dealing with theirs, my one started yelling wildly. I was twisting his arm sharply behind his back. Two big hulks appeared on the stoep above us.

"*Kom hier, klonkie!*" one growled, starting to bound down the stairs.

I didn't wait and neither did Omar and Billy. We scarpered off faster than the Pony Express chased by a stream of Apaches. Our feet pounded like horses' hooves until we judged it safe to slow down and duck into an alley.

"Hey, those Boers nearly had us!" Omar sucked the air between his teeth.

"*Ja!* Ever been hugged by an elephant?" I panted, clasping my ribs. We all laughed to cover up our nerves. Of course, we could have tried to avoid the older boys. We could have used a longer route and zigzagged our way to town, away from the cluster of houses where the "poor whites" lived. But we had our pride. Besides, our narrow escapes were exciting. We had our own enemies, ambushes, and tactics to talk about as well as those of our special heroes.

For a long time Omar, Billy, and I had pooled all

our savings for comics and, when we had enough, for a Saturday matinée. Half the fun was checking every detail of the film afterward. We remembered scenes we had seen months earlier. The Lone Ranger was our clear favorite. So when Mommy began making a cowboy suit just like the Lone Ranger's for the son of one of her white customers, I was jealous.

"Please, Mommy, can't you make me one as well?" I begged.

"When will I have the time? Can't you see all this here for sewing? And these things here for mending? And all this to pack before we move!" Mommy swept one arm around our small living room. A heap of material and another of clothes were stacked on the sofa. A pile of cartons stood by the door. "I'm racing against the clock!"

"*Ag* please, Mommy! I'll do anything you want! I'll help you pack. I'll wash potatoes. I'll—"

Mommy gave me one of her "leave it now" looks. Her warning signal. I watched for a few moments as her right hand coaxed and twirled the brass wheel of her Singer sewing machine. With her left, she steered the brown material under the needle as expertly as the Lone Ranger might guide his trusty Silver through a narrow ravine. Swallowing my pleas, I squeezed between Mommy's chair and the boxes to go outside on to our stoep.

"Just check with Mrs. James that Lisa's all right!" Mommy called after me.

I leaned over the stoep wall to peer into our neighbor's backyard. Lisa and Mrs. James's grandson were playing with a cardboard box as a cart. There was no sign of Wolfie. Mrs. James must have locked him up. I think she had felt sorry for Mommy and offered to help by looking after Lisa. Since my sister was playing happily, I decided there was no need for me to go across to Mrs. James. Instead I jumped up on to the stoep wall, swinging my legs over the edge. It was a good lookout point, and I still couldn't really believe that this wasn't going to be my lookout and my territory forever.

We were one of the first families who were leaving. The Boers who were in charge of the government wanted Jo'burg to be all "white." Everyone who wasn't white in our neighborhood had to clear out. I looked down our road. Our block had houses with red tin roofs and steps leading up from the pavement to each stoep. But the block to the left was crammed with shops. People lived in between, behind, and on top of them. From our stoep I could see the flickering FISH & CHIPS neon sign on one corner and ABC BAZAAR: SPECIALISTS IN RUGS, BLANKETS AND SHAWLS painted in large red letters on a balcony opposite. You could get almost anything down our road, and that end was often jammed with cars until late at night. The pavements were always busy with shoppers, hawkers, people walking by or just hanging around with friends. Sometimes Mommy complained it was like the Tower of Babel with so many different languages, but I loved it. The streets in Coronationville—where we had to go—were boring. It was a township only for Coloreds, and you only heard English and Afrikaans there. Down our street there was always music. Often it was from a scratchy Gramophone or a radio, or it could be someone singing or the Imam calling Moslems from the top of his mosque. Some black kid might come blowing his pennywhistle or you could hear some guys twanging their guitars, trying to copy Elvis. What would our road be like when the whites took it? I had never seen any of the poor whites who lived near us do much work. They couldn't even prevent their own fences and gates from sagging. How would they manage all these shops and everything else? Why should we have to move? This place was home. It just didn't make sense.

"They're rounding us up and fencing us in!" Mommy had grumbled. "They like our work, but why must they push us away so far?"

Pa had managed to remain his calm, quiet-tempered self.

"It's no use winding yourself up," he had said to Mommy. "You'll just give yourself a heart attack. It's just lucky we've only been renting all along. Think of our neighbors who worked themselves to the bone to buy their homes! They're the ones who will really lose out."

That was so like our Pa. To think of someone worse off. But it didn't seem to help Mommy feel any better. Since my little sister was born, Mommy had been working from home as a seamstress. She had white customers and went to their houses to collect and deliver orders. It would be much further for her to travel to her customers from the Colored township. For myself, I would have to change schools, but frankly that didn't bother me.

I didn't think the teachers in one school would be much different from another. Billy's family was also coming to Coronationville so we would still be together. The person I would really miss was Omar. His parents had been told to go to an area much further away that was just for Indians. Omar, Billy, and I had been a threesome for as long as I could remember. I couldn't imagine what it would be like not to spin around together any more. To make ourselves feel better, we promised that we would still meet up. No matter how many miles the government pushed us apart! Just how we would manage this was left for the future.

The person in our house who most definitely refused to stick up his hands and give in quietly, however, was Uncle Richard. He had been a teacher in Cape Town, and when he had lost his job, he had come to live with us in Jo'burg. Uncle Richard had black friends, and I knew that losing his job was something to do with that. Once, two of his black friends called on him at our house. Uncle Richard was upset because Mommy didn't invite them in and they didn't call again. We didn't have a spare room so Uncle Richard shared mine. He was Pa's younger brother and had the same deep brown watchful eyes, but Pa was taller, darker, and spoke a lot more softly. Uncle Richard was more like one of those firecrackers that surprise you because just when you think they've finished, they spark off again. Pa would usually listen quietly, but sometimes Mommy would try to smother him and then end up getting more hot and bothered herself. They even argued over words. When Mommy talked about the "natives," Uncle Richard tried to correct her.

"Look, we're all natives because we were all born in South Africa! Black people call themselves Africans. What's wrong with that? Why must you follow what the white people say?"

Mommy replied that Uncle Richard's mouth always got him into trouble, and if he didn't watch it, he would end up getting us into trouble too.

But Uncle Richard hated how the government was big on sorting everyone into groups. Everyone had to have an Identity Card with their group's name stamped on to it. Uncle Richard said they wanted to stop Coloreds from "playing white" and passing as one of them.

"They should have a proper look in the mirror themselves! What kind of pure human would they

see? *Hmmmhh!*" Uncle Richard was a master of the
scornful snort. Afterward he would inhale deeply
on his pipe, almost closing his eyes. As if he was
trying to wipe the people in charge completely out
of his mind.

Of course he couldn't. From Uncle Richard I
knew that another of their laws was to stop black
and white people from getting married and having
children. In fact, making more Coloreds like us.
Uncle Richard said what else would you expect
from people who wanted Hitler to win the war?
But he also said that all this talk about the Boers
starting apartheid was rubbish. He said the
English had been helping them all along to make
the rope to tie up black people and us Coloreds.
The Boer government was just making new knots
to pull the rope tighter.

"*Hek!*" he used to say. "White people have had
the noose around all our necks ever since your
great-grandpa's people sailed from over the seas
with their bibles and your great-grandma's people
had the land. Now his people have the land, her
people got the bible, and we, in the middle,
landed in the ditch!"

It was from Uncle Richard, and not from Pa,

that I knew that their own grandpa had come from Europe and their grandma from Africa. He was white and she was black. Pa and Mommy didn't talk much about such things. In fact, if Mommy were around, she would interrupt him.

"Stop it, Rich! Don't you be stuffing Jacob's brains with all this politics! He'll end up like you. With no job and a cracked head!"

Ever since Uncle Richard had come home one evening with a blood-soaked bandage wrapped around his skull, "cracked head" had become one of Mommy's favorite sayings. Police with batons had charged into the hall in town where he had been attending one of his political meetings. The cops had broken up the meeting and a few heads as well, including Uncle Richard's. The wound had healed, but Mommy wasn't letting the matter drop. She was always warning Pa's younger brother that he was "cracked" to think that he and his friends could change the government's mind by fighting talk.

But Uncle Richard would just gently finger the left side of his forehead and smile.

"*Ag*, Sis, one day you Coloreds who keep praying that Brother Whitey will invite you to eat at his table will realize that the drawbridge to his castle was pulled up a long time ago! The only place he'll have you is toiling in his kitchen with our black brothers."

Uncle Richard could say the most fiery words but end them with a dry laugh and stay cool. That made Mommy even madder. Often she ended her argument by suddenly clamming up. Her face would fix into grim silence. But whatever she was doing, she would do it more loudly. So we would hear pans banging, water swirling, china rattling, or the iron thumping.

Although there had been months of talk about our removal, it still came as a shock when Pa announced that he wasn't waiting for the government to send its trucks and herd us away like cattle. A friend had offered to bring a delivery van to help us move to the house in Coronationville. That's when Mommy started panicking about finishing her orders on time. The school holidays had begun, and this was the time when she usually complained that either I was under her feet or that she was worried I would get into mischief with Omar and Billy. To make matters worse for me, it was going to be my tenth birthday just the day before Pa's friend was to come with his van. Although they never made a big fuss about birthdays, Mommy and Pa had always given me a present and a little treat to make the day special. I had even been dropping hints about a cap gun that I had seen in Solly's Seconds on the way to town. So when Pa revealed his plans for our move, I tried to remind him about my birthday. He had looked at me sternly and told me that at ten I was entering double figures and nearly grown up. Couldn't I see what a difficult time it was for everyone in the family, especially for Mommy? Then to add to my bad luck, Mommy started making the Lone Ranger suit just like the one I had always wanted— but for somebody else's son!

I don't know for how long I sat dangling my legs over the stoep wall. My little sister and her playmate were no longer out in the backyard, but I was still dreaming and thinking when Omar and Billy appeared on the pavement below me. I hadn't even seen them coming.

"Hands up! Got you covered!"

Omar closed one eye, fixing me in the sights of his finger pistol. Billy leaped up the front steps

ready to pull my arms behind me. I began to struggle, flinging myself back with such force on to the
stoep and pulling Billy down with me. I could see
the surprise in his eyes as he realized I was about
to thrash him.

"Hey pal, cool it!" Omar's voice reached me. His
hands no longer made a pistol but were waving
frantically like flags. He looked so worried and
comic at the same time that my flare of anger van-
ished as swiftly as it had whipped me up.

"What's going on here?" Mommy's voice cut as
sharp as her scissors. "I thought I asked you to
check on your sister."

Omar and Billy both looked embarrassed.

"Sorry, Mrs. Peters," they stumbled.

I bit my lip, confused at my stupidity. I had no
idea why I had caused such a row and right within
Mommy's earshot.

"You, young man," Mommy said, eyeing me,
"had better come inside and start packing."

For the next couple of days, Mommy kept me busy.
First it was cleaning and scrubbing. I couldn't see
why she was so bothered, especially since she kept
our house spotless anyway.

"But we're leaving, Mommy. Why must we worry?" I protested.

"I'm not having those whites saying we left the place dirty."

"But Mommy—"

"No buts. Just do it!" When Mommy had made up her mind, it was like concrete.

Later, when she was ready to deliver her orders, she took me with her to help carry the parcels. It was the day before my birthday although I was trying to put it out of my mind. We set off early in the morning. First there was a long walk to the bus stop and then a long wait under the sign for NON-WHITES . . . NIE BLANKES. Already, there was a thick queue of people ahead of us, mostly black women. A couple had little babies wrapped in blankets, tied to their backs. I had heard Uncle Richard saying that the government was only doing to us now what it had done to the black people before. Pushing them all out of Jo'burg and making them travel for hours and hours to get to work. We watched as three empty buses rumbled past us, stopping for a handful of people at the white bus stop a little way down the road. When I was younger and had come with Mommy on her rounds, we had been allowed to sit upstairs at the back of those white buses. Now things had changed.

I didn't like the trudging up and down roads that stretched like elastic, but I was curious to see at whose house we would deliver the Lone Ranger suit. Maybe I would see the boy Mommy had made it for. Perhaps he was having a birthday too, and it was going to be a surprise. We walked down a broad tree-lined road where the grounds of each house could have swallowed up four or five houses along our street. At last Mommy stopped outside one with a white brick wall and a fancy metal gate. As she lifted the latch, two huge golden-haired dogs bounded across a lawn as smooth as a carpet. Their tongues hung out, and their teeth flashed as they barked. An old black man in blue overalls was carrying a hosepipe to a bed of roses. He turned and waved to Mommy. I clung close to her.

"*Ag*, don't be scared! They know me," Mommy said. "These two will just bark."

Before we even reached the front door, it opened. A boy, about my age, frowned at us. He wore a cowboy hat and, around his waist, a belt with a gun in the holster.

"Why were you so long, hey Betty? I've been waiting forever!" His voice had the kind of whine that I knew got on Mommy's nerves. He hadn't even greeted us, but Mommy just smiled.

"Is your mother in?"

"Mom! Betty's here! At last!" the boy shouted over his shoulder.

The front door opened into a large empty hallway. The only furniture seemed to be a small table on which stood a dark-green potted plant with great leaves like elephant ears. The black and white tiles on the floor shone like marble. We heard the click of heels, and a white lady in a pale-pink suit appeared behind the boy. Her honey-colored hair was fixed as perfectly as if she was a film star.

"Good morning, Betty!" Her voice stalked slowly like my teacher's when he was getting ready to pounce. "Whatever has kept you? I very nearly asked somebody else to make the cowboy outfit!"

"Sorry, Madam. Just too much to do! We have to—"

"Timothy has been asking every day about his suit. You must know how children are." She shook her head and sighed before turning to me. "Is this your son?"

I looked away at the dogs and the garden. I could feel the boy Timothy staring down at me too and my blood rising. He wasn't tough and threatening like the white boys on the way to town, and given half a chance, I could easily have thrashed him. Even before I had actually seen him, I had been jealous. But from the moment I heard him call Mommy "Betty," I disliked him fiercely. When Mommy was asked to go inside to check that the suit fitted properly, I stayed outside. I didn't want to see this pretend Lone Ranger all dressed up! But as Mommy fastened the gate behind us on our way out, he came galloping across the lawn with one of the dogs on a lead and twirling his pistol in the air. The second dog chased alongside, wild with excitement.

"Hi-yo, Silver! Time to hit the trail!" the boy yelled.

Mommy had even made him a mask to complete the outfit.

When we returned home, hot and stiff, Mommy told me to peel the potatoes while she went over to

Mrs. James to collect Lisa. I wanted to protest, but I knew she was as tired as me and that she had to get dinner ready for when Pa came home from work. There was still so much to do, she complained, to be ready for Pa's friend and his van on Saturday. I imagined spending my last day in Jo'burg—my birthday—helping Mommy pack and not with my friends.

Pa was late coming home. After putting Lisa to bed, Mommy gave up waiting and served our dinner.

"He promised to help tonight, and he's not even here," I heard her grumble to Uncle Richard afterward in the kitchen.

But an hour later her voice was much more worried.

"What can have happened, Rich? He's never this late."

Uncle Richard had just offered to investigate by walking to the station when Pa stepped through the doorway. His face looked as heavy as a storm cloud. Mommy made him sit down.

It was the police. At the station exit. But it wasn't one of their usual pass raids herding up black men to inspect their pass books, handcuffing the unlucky and the forgetful. No, this time it seemed they were singling out the men they thought were Colored. They had demanded Pa's certificate, and Pa had asked, "What certificate?" He was told not to play the fool. Since he didn't have a "Population Registration Certificate," they said he had to present himself within twenty-four hours at the Pass Office for classification! A special office had been set up, and a team of officials had come especially to Johannesburg to start the classification. The police took details of where Pa worked so as to check up on him in a couple of days.

"Didn't you tell them? We're already moving to Coronationville? What more do they want? And tomorrow—of all days!" Mommy exclaimed.

"I told you!" Uncle Richard said bitterly. "What they started on black people would come to us."

I thought my uncle was going to make one of his speeches, and there would be another argument. But instead he asked Pa quietly what he was going to do.

"I must go tomorrow," said Pa. He was sure the police would make trouble with his employer if he ignored them.

Pa had never missed a day off work and Mr.

Coley, the factory manager, had to be told that he would be unavoidably late. Pa insisted on going back out to use the telephone at Omar's father's shop. It would still be open. He knew the white suburb where Mr. Coley lived so he could find the number in the directory. He hoped the manager would not mind being disturbed at home, but it was better than finding Pa absent in the morning. Mr. Coley relied on him. We all knew that, from Pa's factory stories.

"Why does Pa need a certificate, Mommy?" I asked as soon as Pa and Uncle Richard had left.

"Take these and pack everything in your cupboard," Mommy said in a voice that was strangely low. "Then I want you to go to bed. It's getting late."

I would have to ask Uncle Richard to get an answer to my question.

When I opened my eyes in the morning, I reminded myself that I was now ten. With everything upside down in our house, who else would remember? I found all the grown-ups at the table, including Pa. On weekdays, he usually left long before I was awake. From the discussion, I gathered

that Mr. Coley had given Pa the day off. Pa promised that he would come home straight after he
had finished at the Pass Office to help Mommy. If
he got there early, he thought he might even be
back before noon.

"We'll manage, Betty. You'll see," Pa said with
his quiet confidence. Mommy raised her eyebrows
and Uncle Richard sat with his arms folded, sucking on his pipe. Pa got up and came toward me.

"Happy birthday, son."

He put his arm around me, and I grinned. He
hadn't forgotten! Then both Mommy and Uncle
Richard wished me a happy birthday. Mommy said
that because I had helped her so much over the
past two days, I could spend the day playing with
Omar and Billy. Mrs. James was going to look after
Lisa, so I could enjoy the whole of my last day with
my friends. Uncle Richard pulled half a crown out
of his pocket. It was mine to buy comics, whichever
I liked! I knew he meant *The Lone Ranger* even
though he liked to tease me about my hero.

When Omar, Billy, and I held our powwow in Billy's
backyard, we all agreed that our last day together
should be something special to remember. Not just

a day of talking about other people's adventures in comics or even our favorite films. I had already told them about Pa being stopped by the police and how he had to report to the Pass Office. It was Billy's idea to track him down there.

"You said your Pa was going to get you that cap gun! So we surprise him when he comes out! We walk home with him past Solly's, and you remind him. He buys it for you, and then we spin around with it!"

It seemed like a good plan. Tracking Pa was part of the adventure. I had heard him mention President Street. Pretending that we were detectives on a case, we made a game out of watching people as we walked. We imagined crimes and discussed the meaning of every twitch, scratch, or flickering eyelid of each of our suspects.

We were having fun until we saw the Pass Office. I had passed it before but never taken too much notice. Men were lined up on the pavement in a queue that stretched all the way along the side of a fat dirty-looking building. They looked tired, like prisoners of war. All of them were black. I knew from Uncle Richard that his black friends hated the little book they had to carry everywhere they went. It had to be signed by a white man who decided where they could live and work. As if they were work animals to be kept chained and branded with their owner's label, said Uncle Richard.

But where would Pa have gone inside the Pass Office? One of us would have to go up to the door and look. Omar and Billy both agreed that it should be me. They would keep watch from the opposite side of the road. As I neared the entrance I suddenly felt nervous. What if Pa was angry that we had followed him? Then he certainly wouldn't get me my cap gun. But it was too late now to change the plan. I slowed down at the entrance, trying not to be put off by the dozens of eyes now on my back. As I peered around the corner of the doorway, I got a shock. A black policeman was standing just on my right. My fingers could have touched the baton hanging from his belt! He was looking straight ahead and hadn't seen me yet. I had to force myself to stay rooted while I quickly scanned what seemed like hundreds of faces inside. My heart was pumping like a frantic piston. I couldn't see Pa anywhere, but there was a corridor on the far side leading away to other doors. The policeman began to jiggle his knee. I swiveled and ran.

We set up watch on the opposite side of the street. We took turns to be the lookout. Omar had his brother's old wristwatch and announced the end of each twenty-minute duty. I told my friends that I was sure Pa could not be too long. The queue for Coloreds was surely shorter than the one that stretched outside. But when each of us had been on duty twice and two hours had passed, we began to feel discouraged. Each hour that passed was an hour less to play with the gun. Once again I was sent across the road into enemy territory to look for any signs of Pa. There weren't any. Had he actually left the building and one of us had missed him?

I was into my third round of duty, and Omar and Billy were beginning to get restless. I was also feeling hungry, wishing I had eaten some of Mommy's porridge. Billy suggested we spend some of my half a crown on chips. I was reluctant to eat into my comic money and was hoping to delay when Pa appeared in the Pass Office doorway. He stepped out very slowly with a piece of paper held in front of him. He wasn't really looking where he was going. His feet seemed to be feeling their own way like those of a blind man.

"Pa-a!"

I heard my own voice. Thin and high like it had been squeezed through a sieve. Pa didn't look up. I darted in front of a bicycle to get across the road.

"Pa? You OK, Pa?"

My father didn't look at me. His gaze was tied to the piece of paper. There was a blankness in his face that scared me, as if he didn't understand what was written. His head was now shaking ever so slightly, and his hand with the paper was trembling. I touched his sleeve lightly with my fingers. Pa glanced at me but didn't seem really to see me because his eyes steered back to the paper. I was aware of Omar and Billy behind me and that people were watching us. I didn't know what to do. Pa seemed to be in a daze. Then an old black man with stubbly gray hair and a face crisscrossed with furrows left the queue and took Pa by the arm.

"Come, *umfowethu*. Come, my brother. Rest here."

Gently, he led Pa to the other side of the door, away from the crowd. He eased Pa against the wall and looked gravely at me. His eyes seemed as old as a hundred winters.

"Let him rest here. Then you take your father home."

I nodded, too shaken to thank him.

Pa didn't speak all the way home. I held his hand while Omar and Billy followed a short distance behind us. I think they were embarrassed. As we passed Solly's I couldn't help glimpsing into the window. The cap gun was still there but, of course, none of us said anything. When we came to Omar's dad's shop, Billy said they would see me later, but it wasn't his usual jokey "See you later, kid!" I felt strangely hollow.

As we passed Mrs. James's house, Wolfie chased us with his usual yapping and the net curtains flickered. I would have let Pa's hand go, but his fingers were tightly wound through mine. We climbed our steps. Through the open doorway I could see more boxes piled on top of each other. Mommy and Uncle Richard had been busy. Mommy poked her head round the kitchen door. She must have seen me first.

"You're early!"

Then she saw Pa.

"What's the matter?" she cried, searching his face.

Her eyes flicked down to the paper in Pa's hand.

"What did they say, Joe?" Mommy's voice was suddenly hushed, and she pulled out a chair for Pa.

"Fetch your uncle!" Mommy pointed in the direction of our bedroom. As I turned around, I saw, in the middle of the packing boxes, the table laid out for a small party. Crisps, my favorite jelly beans, chocolate biscuits, and, in the middle, a cake with candles and a silver paper Happy Birthday. I drew my breath.

"Hurry!" Mommy's hand propelled me from behind.

But Uncle Richard had already heard us. He squeezed his way through furniture and packages straight to Pa and took the piece of paper. Mommy and I trained our eyes on his face. Pa hunched forward, his head in his hands.

"Rejected?" Uncle Richard's voice rose. "What damn nonsense is this? 'Joseph Peters is rejected for registration as a Colored!'"

Mommy's hand flew to her mouth. She lowered herself unsteadily on to a chair next to Pa. For a few moments she sat very still while Uncle Richard read the paper again.

"What does it mean, Uncle Richard?" I asked.

"They want to classify your Pa as an African."

"But . . ."

My head swarmed with "buts." I knew very well from everything Uncle Richard had said before that however bad things were for Colored people, they were much worse for Africans. The queue of tired, hunched figures outside the Pass Office was fresh in my mind. If the Boers said Pa was an African, they wouldn't let him live with us! They would send him away!

"You'd better go and play with your friends while we talk," said Mommy. Two days ago Mommy said I needed to grow up. Now she wanted to protect me again.

"No, let him hear." Uncle Richard put an arm around me.

"*Ja!*" In a soft, low voice, Pa finally broke his silence. "Let him hear."

Pa told us what had happened. He had been taken into an office where a white man had spoken to him in Afrikaans. Pa had answered in the Boer's language, thinking he might make the man angry if he answered in English. Two black policemen were ordered to take Pa's fingerprints. Again, Pa didn't resist. The white man took the fingerprint form and asked Pa a lot of questions. What race was he? Where was he born? To whom was he married? What was his wife's maiden name? What race was his father? What race was his mother? Where did he live? What was his home language? So many questions Pa had forgotten them all. Then the white man had examined Pa.

"Like I was a horse," said Pa.

It was the first time that I heard him sound bitter.

"I told him our grandpa was from Europe. But he said where was my proof? I said they didn't keep papers in those days. Then he asked me, 'If you put milk in coffee, what happens?' I said, 'It remains coffee, but it changes color.' He said, 'Yes, it remains coffee and you are like that.' He just gave me this piece of paper and told me to go."

We were all stunned into silence. I stared at the paper with the scrawling ink. The message on a poisoned arrow.

"You can appeal." Uncle Richard's voice was softer than usual. "My friends know a lawyer who handles these things."

For the first time Mommy didn't make any comment about Uncle Richard's friends being "cracked."

"In the meantime, don't let this get to your manager," he added.

Pa nodded grimly. The workers that Pa supervised were Coloreds. An African would never be allowed to supervise Coloreds! Pa would lose his job. Mommy rested one hand lightly on Pa's shoulder.

"We better have our tea. Then we have to finish this packing."

Mommy sent me to get my sister from next door while she made the tea. When we returned, Mommy, Pa, and Uncle Richard were already squashed around the table. Lisa clambered on to Pa's lap, and Mommy signaled me to sit in front of the cake. As she lit the candles, she tried to force a smile.

"Make a good wish before you blow these out."

The flames flickered and my little sister began to sing "Happy Birthday." We all watched her, and Pa even bounced his knee like a mechanical seesaw. When her little song stumbled to an end, I took a deep breath and blew. I closed my eyes. This wishing game was just make-believe but my wish was desperate.

When I opened my eyes there was a parcel in front of me. I had a present after all.

"Open it," urged Mommy. "Perhaps it will make

your wish come true."

How could it? I felt no excitement. Everything about this birthday was now wrong. My fingers fumbled with the ribbon and paper. The Lone Ranger's outfit—suit and mask—tumbled on to my knees. Exactly the same as Mommy had made for the white boy.

"Don't you like it?" she asked. Her voice was flat. She must have worked late at night when I was asleep. On top of everything else.

"Thanks, Mommy."

The words trotted out, but I didn't feel anything. If I had been given the suit in the morning, I would have been crazy with joy. I would have wanted to show it off straight away to Omar and Billy, like the white boy galloping around his garden. Three hours had changed all that. I suddenly felt much older. Too old for a childish outfit. And for the first time I felt I knew what Uncle Richard meant by the "noose around all our necks."

ONE DAY, LILY, ONE DAY

1 9 6 0

When I was six, policemen snatched Daddy away in the middle of the night. They came to our house with banging, thumping, and shouting. Their flashlights swooped over the garden through the dark. Honey was barking wildly. At first I thought it was a nightmare and cried for Mommy, but when she didn't come, I ran to my parents' bedroom. Daddy was stooped over the bed, surrounded by men in long coats and dark hats. He was packing a suitcase. My brother, Mark, stood barefoot in his pajamas, staring from the corridor outside. He was very silent and I stood beside him, sobbing enough for the two of us. Mommy kept weaving in and out of the policemen to pass Daddy his clothes, his toothbrush and paste, his facecloth. When she held out his razor, a policeman stopped her.

"Forbidden," he grunted through his moustache that was thick as a carpet brush.

Mommy looked more white-faced than Daddy. I wanted to hug him good-bye, but the policemen moved like a wall around him. They bundled him out of the front door into the back of a car. A policeman jumped in either side, trapping Daddy between them. He couldn't even turn his head around to look at us standing on the front doorstep.

Janey, our African maid, was standing in the shadows at the side of the garage next to her room. The car headlights caught her in their glare and her hand shot up to cover her eyes. The tires crunched slowly down the drive until the car reached the gate. Then it roared away into the dark. Honey was still barking crazily from the kitchen yard. The dogs down the road answered her in a chorus. It was Daddy who took Honey out for her early morning run, and she seemed to know that something awful had happened. I stood on our steps clutching on to Mommy with a terrible fear. If those men could just walk into Mommy and Daddy's bedroom and grab him away, they could do anything they liked.

Later, Mark told me that the police might come and take Mommy too. Mommy held me on her lap and said they wouldn't, but really she just said that to make me feel better. She often helped Daddy in his study. The door would be closed, but I could hear them talking and the typewriter tapping. They went to lots of meetings, and sometimes people came to talk with them in the study. Some were family friends who had known me and Mark since we were babies, like Uncle Max. He used to sit me on his shoulders when I was small. It was like being on top of a huge tree. Uncle Max's strong brown arms were the branches, ready to catch me if I fell off. Once, I remember that I cried and cried for Uncle Max to take me on his shoulders to the park to see if I was taller than the slides. He said he couldn't.

"But Daddy takes me," I protested.

"One day, little Lily, one day. When we have freedom, you and I will go to the park."

His voice was so grave that I calmed down, but I still didn't understand that Uncle Max wasn't allowed to take me—a little white girl—to the park because he was black. When the police took Daddy away, I didn't understand that as well.

I didn't say anything in school about Daddy being in jail. My teacher never said a word either, but I felt she knew. It was like a big unspoken. When Janey collected me after school, I could feel the mothers watching us as we walked down the road.

"Do you think they know my daddy is in jail?" I asked Janey.

"They know, Lily. People like to talk."

I let Janey take my hand even though I didn't usually do that anymore.

"Do they think Daddy did something bad?"

"Don't worry what they think," Janey squeezed my palm and stopped to gaze at me directly. Her warm brown face and steady eyes were comforting. "Your daddy is good. Look how he helps other people. Like Busi! He stayed up the whole night to make her better. We'll never forget what he did."

Busi was Janey's favorite niece. She was the same age as me, and when we were four, Busi got a raging fever. Daddy drove all the way to the township with Janey to bring her to the hospital where he worked. Afterward he brought her home to stay with us until she was better. We played every day, and in the end Busi even learned to swim in our pool. I cried when Janey took her back to the township. I wanted her to stay forever.

When they took Daddy to jail, Caroline was already my best friend at school. To be truthful, she was my only friend. We had shared a double-desk since we started. Our Grade One teacher said we reminded her of the sisters Snow White and Rose Red. Caroline's hair was silky and fair while mine was thick and dark. Her eyes were dove blue and mine were olive green. Her mom used to give me a tight little smile whenever she saw us holding hands as we came out of the gates. It was ages before I was invited to their house—after my seventh birthday—and whenever I asked Caroline to come to mine, her mom used to say that Caroline was going out with them and they were busy.

"Are you really busy?" I asked one time.

"I think my mommy doesn't like your daddy because he's in jail," Caroline whispered.

"No, he's not!" I protested. "My daddy came home long ago! Tell your mommy that."

Caroline didn't have any other special friends, and, in the end, I was invited over. I was on my very best behavior. At teatime I made sure not to talk with my mouth full and not to speak unless spoken to. When Caroline's mother asked me about Janey, I wished I didn't have to speak at all.

"That girl who gets you after school—she always looks a bit cheeky to me—has your mommy had her for a long time?" She was smiling her tight smile again. Her question was like a hook, and I was her little fish. I hated the way she called Janey a "girl" and "cheeky." I wished I could tell her "My parents say it's rude to talk about Africans like that!" But I didn't. Instead I nodded and said, "Yes, she has."

"Well at least they brought Lily up to be polite!" I overheard Caroline's mom say to her dad afterward. I wanted to turn around and scream, "What do you think? Do you think we're animals?" I should have said, "What about *you* being polite about Janey?" But I didn't. Even with her horrible parents, I wanted Caroline to be my friend.

After my first visit, Caroline must have nagged so much that her mom finally let her come to my house. They didn't have a pool in their garden like we did, and I think Caroline went on about it. She was also desperate to see Honey's puppies. We were so excited, whispering in class about our plans, that we were each given a hundred lines in ink: "I must not talk in class unless my teacher asks me a question." We had to spend a whole lunchtime writing them at opposite ends of the classroom. Our teacher said she would know if we talked even though she was in the staff room. So we made silent signs to each other, flicking our fingers like sparklers every time we completed another ten.

Mommy had agreed to a Saturday when there wasn't a meeting at our house. We had a great time. We cuddled the puppies, swam, and played hide-and-seek in the garden. We groaned when Caroline's parents arrived to collect her. Daddy invited them in for a beer, and they hovered on the doorstep looking awkward.

"That's sounds good if . . ." Caroline's dad seemed ready to accept. Caroline and I pinched each other's hand, hoping we'd get more time to play. But her mom's red lips stretched as wide as a Venus flytrap.

"Thank you—it's a shame we don't really have time today! We're actually on our way somewhere else."

After that, however, we went to each other's house a lot. Mostly, I was invited to Caroline's. Her mom said she knew my parents were busy people, although really I think she thought it safer to have

us under her eye. It suited Mommy that way
because of the work she and Daddy did. There was
only one time when Caroline was visiting that there
was an unexpected meeting at our house. Mommy
called me aside and asked if we would play outside
so as not to disturb the grown-ups. Later Caroline
wanted to go to the bathroom. She returned in a
hurry, her forehead and nose wrinkled.

"There's a strange native inside your house! As
big as a giant!" she panted. "He came out of the
bathroom and went into your dad's study!"

Then she widened her eyes in horror. She loved
to make up dramas.

"Do you think he's a burglar?"

I realized it must be Uncle Max. I bit my lip,
unsure what to say.

"Shouldn't we tell your parents?" Caroline per-
sisted.

I shook my head.

"It's all right. My daddy probably knows him."

"But what's he doing in your house? Is he your
garden boy?" Caroline now looked puzzled.

I didn't explain that Uncle Max was a friend,
not a "boy." Instead I tugged her arm.

"Jeez, I'm hot! Why don't we go in the water

again? Race you there!"

I prayed that Caroline wouldn't say anything to her parents or they wouldn't let her come again. She probably realized this too because at school on Monday we exchanged sandwiches and crisps at playtime as usual. I breathed more easily.

There are two days from our friendship I'll never forget. Our best day ever was on my ninth birthday when Caroline was invited to my birthday treat at the drive-in. My parents were taking us to see a Walt Disney film. My brother thought that *Bambi* was too babyish for him and said he wouldn't come. I was secretly glad. He would have spoiled it all by complaining that we were being silly. Half the fun was having the backseat to ourselves and being free to giggle, gasp, and clutch each other. We oohed and aahed over Bambi and each of his forest friends. Daddy ordered a round of milk shakes, hotdogs, and chips just like all the other families in the rows of cars around us.

"Your stomach has never grown up!" Mommy teased him.

Daddy had us in stitches with his silliest jokes on the way home, and we quizzed each other about which bits of the film we liked best. We decided the little rabbits were just the cutest of all and we would each start a rabbit collection—china ones, posters, pictures—anything with a sweet little rabbit on it. I felt so happy and I think Caroline did too. Like we were up in the air—on a seesaw.

A few months later we crashed down. Our worst day ever. The strange thing is that I can't remember the new girl, Alice, at all that day although I'm sure she must have been somewhere in the middle of it. At break, we saw our principal holding her skirt and running across the courtyard to the staff room. Jeez, what was happening? We all stopped to watch. A minute later, she was dashing back toward her office with two teachers following her. Other teachers hurried across the grounds to the front and back gates. None of us knew what was going on until the rumor started.

"The natives are coming to attack us! They're on their way now!"

There was panic. Someone had overheard the teachers discussing what to do. Should they keep us safe in school or try to contact our parents to come and get us? We whirled around the courtyard like crazy goldfish. Caroline hugged me madly.

"The natives are coming, Lily! Save me, save me!" she squealed.

"What can we do?" I squealed back, pleased to have Caroline hugging me and acting silly just like we had done at the drive-in. As soon as the words were out of my mouth, I felt uncomfortable. Wouldn't Mommy and Daddy be disgusted at how everyone was screaming about "the natives"? But what should I do when Caroline and everyone were shrieking and making me frightened too? I was saved by our principal's voice.

"Attention girls! Line up immediately! In silence, please!"

Caroline let go of my waist and grabbed me by the hand. She gritted her teeth as if something terrifying was about to happen. I had never seen her look so pale as she pulled me to where we Standard Threes lined up. The chattering and screaming had stopped, but a few girls were actually crying. Our teachers looked as worried as mother hens trying to settle us.

Our principal explained that if we were sensible, we would come to no harm. If our parents came to get us early, we would be allowed to leave. No one should go home alone.

"How will you get home?" Caroline whispered urgently on our way back to class.

"Walk." I was sure Mommy wouldn't panic like the other parents. Our house wasn't far and since Standard One I had been walking home by myself.

Caroline looked horrified.

"You can't—and you won't be allowed! It's too dangerous! I'll ask my mom if you can come with us."

I didn't argue. We might be allowed to spend the afternoon together and that would be fun once Caroline had calmed down.

Caroline's mom was one of the first to arrive. She was out of breath and tottered on her high heels from running. Her face was flushed, and her voice was higher and faster. She had heard the news on the radio and wanted Lily safely at home. When Lily asked if I could come too, I thought her mom looked strangely at me for a second before nodding. She made that tight little smile of hers in my direction and turned to our teacher.

"Well, you spoil them, and this is what they do!" Her voice arched upward like her eyebrows as if to carry a special meaning.

Straight away I knew that by "them" and "they" she meant Africans. Not only that, but she was also talking about my parents and their politics. I should have told her and Caroline, "No, thank you," there and then. I should have said that I didn't want their lift. But I didn't.

When we were in the car, I asked Caroline's mom if she could drop me at home.

"Who's at your house? Is your mother there?"

"Janey's there. Mommy will be home later. It's fine."

"Look, I'm not saying your girl can't be trusted, but today's not a normal day. I'd never forgive myself if something happened to you! You'd better come home with us." She gave a loud sigh.

"You'll be safer with us *and* we get to play!" Caroline was bouncing back to her old self.

Why didn't I tell them that Janey had looked after me since I was a baby? Why didn't I tell them that she was one of the safest people I knew? Instead I let Caroline tell me about her new game collection.

Caroline's mom rang Janey to tell her I was with them. I could hear her from the dining room.

"When will your Madam be back? You must tell her to ring me as soon as she comes in. Do you understand?" I'd never heard Mommy talk to

Janey like that. The voice was sharp. Frightening. I felt shivery inside. I suddenly didn't feel like finishing my chocolate cake and pushed it away.

"Are you feeling sick?" Caroline asked. "I feel sick too! I was scared at school, weren't you?"

When I didn't reply, Caroline clapped her hands around her face.

"Oh no! Do you think the natives are still coming?"

I shook my head. I just felt miserable and wanted to be in my own home. Janey would find a way of making me feel better.

"What'll we do if they come here? You won't be able to go home, will you? We'll have to ask my mom if you can stay the night!" Caroline's face switched like a lightbulb—one second scared, the next excited.

She took out her new box of games.

"What shall we start with?"

I let her choose. I couldn't concentrate and let her Ludo counters gobble mine up. Then in draughts all her counters became kings and wiped me off the board. We ended by arguing.

"You're not playing properly, Lily! It's no fun if you don't try."

"I don't feel well. I want to go home."

"You're mad! You heard what my mom said! The natives are dangerous! How come you don't know?"

I kept quiet. Was she holding something back? Something she thought about my parents. The kind of things her parents thought. But she wasn't saying it yet. I too didn't want to fight over parents.

"I've got a headache," I said dully. "Can I lie down?"

Caroline told her mom, and I was taken to the spare room. I must have dozed off because I was startled to find Mommy pressing my arm lightly, waking me up. Caroline and her mom stood in the doorway behind her. Everyone was stiffly polite as we left.

Before we even got to the car, I was telling Mommy about the panic in school. I wanted to tell her also about Caroline's mom and how badly she had spoken to Janey. But she interrupted, putting both hands on my shoulders and looking straight at me.

"A very terrible thing happened today, Lily. Africans weren't marching to Johannesburg at all. They were marching to a police station in the township—to protest about the passes that make their lives a misery—that control where they must live, where they must work—everything. They were marching to the police to say, 'Arrest us if you want to!' But they never even got there." Her voice was choked. Angry. Tears flooded her eyes. She fought them as she fumbled with the key in the car door. She said I would find out more when we got home.

I still don't understand everything that happened that day. Perhaps I never will. But I remember Janey sitting at the kitchen table, staring blankly ahead of her, not even turning toward Mommy and me as we came in. A young man—an African whom I'd never seen before—stood beside Janey, speaking to her in Zulu, their own language. From his face I knew he was describing something awful. Mommy sat down and stretched across the table for Janey's hand, but Janey shrank away. It was only then that it hit me. The township where people had marched to the police station must be the same one where Janey's family lived.

When Mommy asked the young man to tell her what had happened, he spoke in English. He was Janey's cousin and had come to break the news that her brother's child had been shot. She and her friends had been playing near the people who were marching to the police station. There was no warning. The police just began shooting. At first people thought they were firing blanks. Some women even laughed, but then bodies started falling. Everyone was running away, but the police went on shooting. Many people were dead.

"The children—they were leaping like rabbits—over the bodies." The young man bounced the palm of his hand up and down as if to show how the children had leaped.

"It's . . . it's not Busi, is it?" I stuttered.

Janey's eyes turned toward me but seemed to look right through me.

"Yes," Janey's cousin said simply, "it's Busi."

"Is she . . . is she. . . ?" I couldn't say the word.

"The bullet went here." He jabbed at the lower part of his back. "She's crying in the hospital for her aunty."

I ran to Janey and threw my arms around her neck, nestling my tears into her maid's pink uniform. I could feel her chest heaving, but her eyes were dry. I saw Busi leaping like a rabbit as bullets were flying, and I sobbed. I could feel Janey

wanting to get up, and I was clinging on. I heard
Mommy's voice.

"Lily, you must let Janey go. Busi needs her!"

Only when Janey had patted me on my back did
I let her remove my arms and stand up. My
brother Mark hung in the doorway, silent and awkward. Janey had looked after him since he was a
baby too.

Daddy didn't come home that night. He went to
help at the hospital with the injured people. In
school the next day our teachers didn't tell us what
had really happened, and none of my classmates
talked about it. The panic from the day before was
over. It was like it had just been a bit of an adventure. I tried to tell Caroline about Busi and the
children who were shot like rabbits. She thought I
was peculiar.

"Stop it, Lily! You'll give me nightmares! My
mom doesn't let me listen to anything like that—
she knows what I'm like."

If I had never tried to tell Caroline about Busi, I
wonder if we would still be best friends? We didn't
ever have a real quarrel or proper fight. We just
stopped going off alone together at break and
stayed with the other girls instead. We didn't talk

about our rabbit collection and didn't say anything about visiting each other at the weekend. Perhaps we both wanted to forget a little before starting over again. But nine days later something else happened that would have split us anyway like a huge chopper. . . .

After the shooting in Janey's township, the demonstrations spread like wildfire all over the country. The government made a State of Emergency, and Daddy was arrested again. The police said they were locking up the "troublemakers." It didn't make sense. Did they really think Daddy started the trouble? His picture was in the newspaper with Uncle Max's and lots of other people who had been thrown into jail.

It was Alice, the new girl, who broke the Big Unspoken in school: Don't mention Lily's parents in front of her. I should have expected that someone would say something but still she caught me by surprise with her loud, brassy voice.

"My mom says your parents are Commies. She says they have native friends. Is it true they sit and eat with you?"

My cheeks flushed red hot. A hush swept through the children lining up outside our classroom. I felt everyone watching, waiting. Alice's cat-green eyes bore into me. A stony face like the Sphinx with plaits on either side. Was it best to remain silent? But a nervous giggle behind me, sounding suspiciously like Caroline, unlatched my mouth and a reply just popped out.

"Well, your parents have dinner every day with a monkey. You!"

Without waiting for our teacher to arrive—and with my head high—I stepped out of the line and strode into the classroom: Alice's voice followed me in a whine.

"I was only telling the truth, wasn't I, Caroline?"

I covered my ears. I didn't want to hear the reply from someone who had been my one and only best friend.

I hate Alice and her sneering over Mommy and Daddy. What does she know? I think she and Caroline are becoming best friends. I see them whispering together, and I think they're talking about me. I miss Caroline most at weekends. Mark won't play with me. If he isn't playing cricket or rugby, he's moody and locks himself in his room.

Mommy knows that things have changed

between Caroline and me, but we haven't really spoken about it. It's four months now since Daddy was arrested, and I know Mommy worries about him all the time even though she tells us he will be fine. Every day she goes to the jail to take food, clean clothes, and collect his washing.

Sometimes I feel so mixed-up and angry. Nasty, stupid thoughts come into my head. Like why couldn't Mommy and Daddy be like the other parents who don't bother with politics and don't care if things aren't fair? What about me and Mark? Don't we matter? I even shouted that the other day at Mommy.

"Of course you matter," she said. "You matter very much. But what about Uncle Max's children? And all the other children in this country—like Busi? Don't they matter too?"

How could I answer that? But at night I lie awake thinking what will happen to Mark and me if the police come and take Mommy away too.

At least Janey is back with us, so I go and sit in the kitchen and do my homework and other things there. We don't talk as much as we used to when I was little, and Janey doesn't like to talk much about Busi now. I overheard her tell Mommy that the whole family is praying that Busi will walk again properly. But the other day Janey asked me about Caroline.

"She's not my friend any more. She's friends with a horrible girl—Alice."

"*Ttch-ttch* . . . shame!" Janey shook her head and quietly went on drying the dishes. I couldn't bring myself to tell her what had happened, but I felt she knew. I turned back quickly to my drawing of mountains, trying to push away thoughts of Alice, Caroline, her mother, and all the rest of them. I felt like scrunching up my paper until I felt Janey's hand resting lightly on my shoulder.

"One day, Lily, it will come right."

"Do you really think so, Janey?"

"I think so, Lily." She slipped her hand away and went back to the dishes. I got on with painting my mountains.

I try to keep Janey's words hanging inside my head now. They remind me of Uncle Max saying "One day, little Lily, one day. When we have freedom, you and I will go to the park." I don't know when one day will be, but I tell myself that if Uncle Max, Janey, Mommy, and Daddy all believe in it, I should try too.

THE TYPEWRITER

1976

"Here, read this! Give it to your parents!"

Someone thrust a leaflet into Nandi's hand. She glanced at it, keeping in step with the steady march of school students on their way to the cemetery.

> **PARENT-WORKERS! DO NOT GO TO WORK ON MONDAY!** We the black students of South Africa have left our schools to fight the oppressors who keep us down. We want to write exams, but not while the police are murdering our brothers and sisters.
>
> Parents, you should be proud to have children who prefer to die from bullets than swallow the poison in our schools.
>
> Parent-workers, hear our call and STAY AWAY FROM WORK ON MONDAY! We have nothing to lose but our chains!

For the last few weeks Nandi's school had been

closed. From the news on Radio South Africa it seemed that all over the country black students were refusing to go to classes. Some schools had even been burnt down. Everywhere the cry was rising, "Down with Bantu education!" "Down with white rule!"

With news of shootings and mass arrests, Nandi's mother worried constantly about leaving her children when she was out at work in the factory. Nandi was eleven and the twins barely three years old. But Ma had no choice, except to ask old Ma Tabane, their neighbor, to keep an eye on them.

Ma had been especially anxious about today. It was to be the funeral of two students from the high school, shot by police a week ago. Before leaving for work early that morning, Ma had told Nandi very firmly, "Don't go out at all. There'll be trouble for sure."

Nandi hadn't wanted to disobey Ma but, when she had heard the shouts and the singing so close to the house, she had felt unable to resist. Her little brother and sister had been playing happily in the backyard. Ma Tabane had been hanging out washing next door, calling over to them occasionally.

She was rather deaf, and her crackly old radio blared out music that seemed to cover the other sounds being carried in the air. Quietly Nandi had slipped out through the front of their small box house and into the dry stony street. With luck, no one would notice she was missing for a short while.

Marching along with hundreds of students, dust rising from under their feet, Nandi now carefully folded the leaflet she had been told to give to her mother, putting it in her pocket. She wasn't sure what Ma would say about it. There was also the problem that if she gave it herself, Ma would know her order had been disobeyed. She would have to ask Esther to pass it on. Her cousin was sixteen. Living with Khulu, their granny, Esther seemed free to do so many things Ma would never let Nandi do. When Khulu went off to work each day to sell fruit in Johannesburg, Esther didn't have to stay at home looking after younger children.

Nandi kept looking for Esther in the crowd. It was certain she was there, probably near the front. The older students usually led the way, carrying homemade banners and hurling their voices into the air. Nandi knew all the freedom songs by now.

Esther and her friends had taught them to her. But this was electric, so many people singing together what they felt:

> *"We are the young people,*
> *We will not be broken!*
> *Come with your cannons,*
> *Come with your guns!*
> *We demand freedom*
> *And say*
> *'Away with slavery,*
> *In our land of Africa!'"*

Nandi's voice mingled with the rest. At least their voices were free. Street after street, past rows of box houses all like her own, hundreds of feet and voices stirred up those who were not working in the city. Faces appeared at doors and windows. Little children ran out shouting before being pulled back by firm elderly hands. A voice from the side rang out,

"Go back home! You youngsters are asking for trouble!"

"Don't worry, Baba! We're ready for it!" someone shouted back.

Another old man, struggling off a chair in his front yard, raised up an arm and fist.

"*Amandla!*" In a wavery, thin voice he called for strength.

"*Ngawethu!* To the people," thundered students passing by, cheering and waving to him.

As they neared the cemetery, however, the mood suddenly changed. A halt in the march brought students packing in on each other. Up ahead, beyond the banners, Nandi could see that the cemetery gates were closed, barred around by rows of police and gigantic gray tanks. Steel monsters with great square black eyes. A voice was barking through a loudspeaker: "YOU ARE TO GO HOME IMMEDIATELY! ONLY FAMILIES OF THE DECEASED MAY ENTER!"

The crowd roared back: "THEY WERE OUR BROTHERS! LET US IN!"

Suddenly a great cry rose up. Choking, coughing, eyes stinging, blinded with something fierce and burning, Nandi found herself being pushed and pulled to avoid the swinging, crashing batons. Stones skimmed overhead toward the police as the school children began to push back desperately, scattering to find cover, fearing more of the terrifying gunshots. The same gunshots that brought them to the cemetery today to sing their songs for the two already dead. Once again, songs had turned to screams and cries. Nandi could hear her own voice ringing out as she ran home. Above it echoed sharp, fearful cracks through the air.

No one saw Nandi slip back into the house. She grabbed her rope and began to skip vigorously out in the front to cover up her shaking. When Ma Tabane came to sweep the dirt out of her front door, she shook her head slightly.

"Ai, Nandi! You'll finish yourself like that!"

Ma came home later than usual. There had been a rush job at the factory, and she had been ordered to work overtime. She knew already there had been trouble at the cemetery.

"You stayed at home?"

Nandi nodded.

"Did Esther come here today?"

"No, Ma."

"*Tch!* That boss has no heart!"

Ma spoke angrily. She looked upon her brother's child as her own and wouldn't be at ease until she knew Esther was safe. But now, with the curfew, it was too late for a half-hour walk through the dark streets of Soweto to Khulu's house. Nandi kept very quiet, trying not to let the pictures in her mind show on her face.

Tap-tap. Tap-tap-tap.

At first it seemed part of her dream that night . . . .

Nandi was acting "lookout" for Esther and her friends as they held a secret meeting in the tiny, cramped kitchen while Khulu and the neighbors were all out at work. Nandi's job was to play outside, but if she saw anyone strange enter the road, she had to warn Esther immediately so the others could slip away through the back. She was pretending to be busy skipping in and out through the gate, when she heard the tapping. It sounded as if the students were typing. Then Nandi realized the rhythm was wrong. She froze. Whatever was it? She wanted to call out a warning signal, but somehow her open mouth had become stiff. . . .

Nandi woke up, feeling panic. The tapping *was* real, coming softly from the window. Then everything was silent for a few seconds, except for the breathing of the twins sleeping next to her. It was very dark, probably after midnight. No noises came from outside now—no running footsteps, no odd shouts or cries, no roaring of police vans.

Nandi gripped her breath and waited.

Tap-tap-tap-tap-tap.

The soft tapping came more rapidly. Her heart drummed as she forced herself from the bed to the window.

"Who is it?" she whispered through the open slit. She clenched the curtain, scared to pull it back.

"It's me . . . Esther! Open quickly!"

Carefully, she released the latch and leaned forward. The shape of her cousin was pressed up against the wall. Eerie moonlight lit part of the yard but the side of the house was in deep shadow. Before Nandi could say anything, Esther began:

"Look, Nandi, I need help!"

"Ah! Are you hurt?"

Esther was shaking, and Nandi could just make out that she was clutching her arm. Her voice was low and hoarse.

"It's nothing . . . later . . . there's something urgent!"

Breathing heavily, the older girl explained. In the afternoon she and her friends had been close to the cemetery gates. Themba and Zinzi had been carrying a banner saying: "THEY DIED FOR FREEDOM."

When the police attacked, both Themba and Zinzi had been grabbed. Esther had escaped, although a baton had whipped down on her arm. She had seen both her friends being beaten about their heads and thrown like sacks into a police van.

Esther feared the worst. Everyone knew the police stopped at nothing to get information. There were funerals to prove it. So it wouldn't be long before they would be coming for her too. Even now, someone could be secretly watching Khulu's house, waiting. . . . But worse, they might have started searching the house—and then Khulu would be in terrible trouble.

"It's the typewriter, Nandi. For our leaflets. I hid it—but if they find it, they'll arrest Khulu. They won't believe she knows nothing!"

Nandi sucked in her breath, horrified. Esther continued.

"It's not only Khulu. That typewriter can send us to jail for a long time."

"Can't we do something? Can't I get a message to Khulu?"

"It's dangerous. Not a game."

"I know . . . but I can try . . . first thing in the morning. If someone is watching the house, I can look as if I'm going to help Khulu."

Esther said quietly,

"It's very risky . . . but it's our only chance. There's no one else I can ask."

"Where is the hiding place?" asked Nandi simply.

Briefly Esther explained that the typewriter was hidden behind the kitchen cupboard, wrapped in brown paper. Nandi and Khulu would have to pull away the panel at the back. To get rid of the package, she said they should stuff it in the dustbin outside the backdoor and cover it well with the rubbish. If the police didn't find it in their search, it might even be possible for a friend to retrieve it later.

"But what if the back of the house is being watched?"

"Then we're trapped," replied Esther.

Although her voice was steady, her cousin was still clasping her arm.

"Where will you go? What about your arm?"

"I'll find somewhere . . . and tell Khulu I'm

sorry. . . ." Esther paused. "It had to be done. Tell her not to worry. I'll send her a message as soon as I can."

Nandi's eyes followed Esther's bent shape making its way across the yard. After closing the window, trying not to let it squeak, she crept back into bed to wait for the morning. She curled herself up small and tight, as if to hold in her fear and stop it from growing.

It was impossible to take her mind off Esther stumbling away into the dark to look for a "safe" house . . . Themba and Zinzi being hit about the head . . . Themba who always greeted Nandi with a wink and his "How's it, sis?" . . . Zinzi with her warm smile and special way of swinging your hand in friendship. Both looked on her as a younger sister. When she had acted as "lookout" for their meetings, she had known it was something serious, yet it had still been a bit like a game. Although she had known there was danger, it was also exciting. But what she had to do this time contained no enjoyment, no excitement of that kind at all. The danger was all around now. When she began to think of Khulu, her mind blocked off. The police couldn't harm her. No, no . . .

Nandi set off at first light, slipping out before her mother was up. She left a note: Gone to Khulu.

Nandi wasn't sure what to tell Ma when she returned. It was too difficult to sort out at the moment. Later, after taking the message, she would think about it.

Gray mist hung over the streets and the early morning air was chilly. Nandi hugged her arms around her as she ran. Already a stream of people were walking steadily toward the station. In the half-light they seemed almost like ghosts, pulled by some invisible cord toward the city. Their grandmother usually set off for work early, so Nandi had to hurry. Perhaps Khulu had gone out looking for Esther. She must be so worried . . . and how would she be on hearing the message . . . angry, upset, frightened? Nandi refused to let herself imagine the police in the house itself.

Along the way Nandi could see the signs of people's fury. The place where Ma came to pay the rent was a heap of smouldering rubble, smoke mingling with the mist. Further on, the roof of the high school was missing, the walls blackened and windows shattered. She ran on, pausing only at one point to press herself against a fence as a police patrol truck thundered past.

Near Khulu's road, out of breath and panting, Nandi stopped to lean against a wall. If the police had set someone to watch the house, her arrival must seem absolutely normal. It was impossible to prevent her heart from throbbing, but once her breathing had slowed down a little, she walked on.

Turning the corner, she saw the strange car immediately. It was parked a little way up the road from the house, with its hood raised and two men bending over the engine. One was holding a flashlight. Perhaps they were genuine and had really broken down. But why so close to Khulu's? How could you know if they were informers? She had heard Esther and her friends discussing walkie-talkies once. What if the flashlight was one?

Nandi had to walk right past, quite casually. Close to the car, she found herself humming the tune of one of the students' songs very softly to herself. It seemed to give her courage. The man with the flashlight glanced directly up at her as she passed. Reaching Khulu's front yard at last, she clicked the gate carefully behind her. With the feeling that eyes were following her, she made her way around to the backdoor, out of sight.

From the moment she had come home the evening before, after her day in Johannesburg, Khulu had known something was wrong. News had begun spreading earlier in the day among the flat workers near where Khulu sold fruit. A mid-afternoon radio report had mentioned "trouble at a funeral." Later, billboards for the evening newspaper had been headlined: "FUNERAL SHOOTING: THREE DEAD."

By the time Sowetans were making their long journey home by train, some had read the first reports. Their comments had weaved rapidly through the tightly crowded carriages. Parents and grandparents had made silent prayers.

Outside the station Khulu had found heavily armed police ordering people to go straight home and stay inside. A great tank had come roaring down the road and up the hill. Smoke and flames had been rising from the direction of the Rent Offices. Balancing her half-filled box of fruit on her head, Khulu had forced her tired body onward. When finally she had found the house empty—and no food prepared—anxiety already burning within her had leaped up like a flame. It was true that sometimes Esther came in late, but there would always be some supper waiting in the pot, prepared by Esther earlier on.

Khulu had wanted to go out looking for her grandchild straight away. Was she one of those shot? Had she been hurt or arrested? She would have to find one of Esther's friends. Yet what if something had happened to them too? Maybe in the end she would have to ask at the police station.

She had just been starting up the road again, when her neighbor's husband had called out to her. Hadn't she heard the police message? They were going to shoot anyone on the streets at night. Khulu had halted. She could hear the rumble of tanks, could see smoke rising in different places, could smell burning in the air. She was not young any more and could not have moved quickly to take cover like the youngsters on the street corners. Wearily she had returned to the empty house, to wait till the morning.

All night Khulu had sat up. When the knocking came early in the morning, she hurried to the door. Could it be Esther at last? Instead, there was

Nandi, almost falling on to her and stammering her message.

What happened next was something that remained for a long time in Nandi's mind like a silent film. Without saying a word, her deeply lined face very grave, Khulu lowered herself with difficulty onto her knees beside the cupboard. Her worn, wrinkled hands passed Nandi two old gray saucepans and a bent frying pan, before the two of them loosened and lifted out the back panel. It was there. Together they pulled out the heavy brown-paper parcel.

"What rubbish can we throw on top?" Nandi whispered.

Khulu signaled for Nandi to wait. She heaved herself up. Then taking the box in which she carried fruit, she tipped out apples, oranges, and bananas onto the bed. Lifting the brown-paper package, she placed it at the bottom of the box and began to pile the fruit on top of it. It was all done in a couple of minutes. There was another small box of fruit on a chair. She pointed to it.

"Bring that!" she said to Nandi.

Nandi was speechless. Whatever was Khulu going to do with the typewriter?

Slowly Khulu raised the large box onto her head, balancing it carefully. Nandi did the same with the small one and followed her grandmother out of the backdoor. Khulu led the way across the small yard to a narrow gap in the back fence. There was a spot in crossing the yard where the men by the car could see them if they were looking in that direction. But there was no sound of footsteps as they reached the back fence. Making their way silently between the opposite houses, they passed out into the next street.

Nandi desperately wanted to ask Khulu what she intended to do, but when she began to speak, Khulu shook her head. So, without knowing where they were going, Nandi followed her grandmother as they walked steadily onward, the boxes swaying gently on their heads.

There were a couple of black policemen standing at the entrance to the station. Nandi's heart jumped as one of them put out a hand and lifted a bunch of bananas out of her grandmother's box.

"Thanks, granny!" he said, tearing off a banana and throwing it to his mate. He didn't offer to pay, but Khulu simply turned to look at him, her grave face giving a slight nod.

Khulu took her usual route to work. The over-crowded train to Johannesburg, then the over-crowded bus to the white suburb with the tall blocks of flats. For the last thirty years she had come six days a week to sell fruit to people hurrying to and from cooking, cleaning, and serving inside the homes of Masters and Madams.

Nandi had come with Khulu before, standing all day from early in the morning until late in the evening, at the corner of a big block of flats near the bus stop. She had seen white people driving off in smart cars, long after Khulu and the other workers had arrived in the morning. She had seen the same white people driving back home, long before Khulu and the other black people set off on their tiring journey home to Soweto.

Nandi had seen white children in expensive uniforms, complete with hats and caps, walking or being driven to school, and coming home in the middle of the afternoon, licking ice creams, laughing. The white children's school couldn't be like her own—of that she was sure, even though she hadn't seen it. In her school there were so many children that her class finished at eleven o'clock so that another lot of children could come in.

This morning as she stood at the same corner, Nandi's mind was in a turmoil. Whenever Esther had spoken about what was so bad in their country, Khulu had usually remained quiet, getting on with her work. Nandi could remember only once how she had put down her iron and said: "You children always want things to happen so quickly! You think you are the first to fight . . . and that it's easy!"

"But, Khulu . . ." Esther had begun.

"No, it's no use telling me. . . . I'm too old!" Their grandmother had shaken her head and started ironing again.

That was why this was so puzzling, startling. . . . Khulu acting so swiftly and calmly . . . bringing the typewriter right into the middle of the white people, almost under the noses of the police. Nandi wanted to ask why Khulu was doing this dangerous thing. Wouldn't it have been so much easier to throw the parcel away into the trash? Each time someone bought an orange, an apple, or a banana, the layer of fruit got less. What did Khulu intend to do now?

Nandi waited for most of the passersby to go into work and the street to quiet down before she whispered her question.

"Khulu, what are you going to do with it?"

Looking at the young worried face, Khulu smiled a little.

"There's a place where it will be safe for a while. . . ." she paused, then added softly, "How can I throw it away when the children still need it?"

Nandi moved up close to Khulu, resting against her, not saying anything more. Words were too difficult.

A little later, when the traffic of passing cars had lessened, Khulu left Nandi standing at the corner with the small box of fruit. Having placed the large box once again on her head, she slowly made her way toward the drive-in entrance to the block of flats. All seemed quiet. Just beyond the entrance archway was a row of garages. The nearest one was open. Biting her lip, Nandi edged herself a little way up the road. Nervously she watched as Khulu strolled through the entrance and stopped by the vacant garage. Inside, Nandi glimpsed a shelf cluttered with old cardboard boxes. After a brief glance around her, Khulu entered. She placed the fruit box down on the floor and carefully lifted out the brown-paper parcel.

At that moment a silver car came swerving around the corner of the street. Nandi stared in dismay. The car swung into the driveway and directed itself toward the very garage where Khulu was wedging the package on to the shelf. A white woman flung open the car door, screaming in English.

"What do you think you're doing? Come in here to steal, have you?" Her fingers pointed like red-tipped missiles.

Khulu shook her head, but didn't reply.

The screech continued. "What's that you've been meddling with then? Let me see!"

Nandi ran toward the entrance, but stopped short as the white woman strode into the garage, pulled down the parcel on to the garage floor and ripped open the paper. There lay the typewriter, next to the box of oranges, apples, and bananas.

"This isn't mine! It's stolen, isn't it? So you've come to hide it in my garage! Well you've been caught my girl!"

By now a small crowd of people had gathered near the garage. A large white man made his way through to the screaming woman. Khulu stood still, saying nothing.

"What's the trouble, Mrs. Laker?"

"It's this thief here. . . ."

At the word "thief," Nandi forgot her own terror and ran to Khulu. She sobbed against her.

"You're not a 'thief,' Khulu! You didn't steal anything! Tell them! Please tell them!"

Khulu's body heaved as she held her granddaughter tightly for a few seconds. Then, from under her shawl, she slipped her little purse with its few coins into Nandi's pocket, saying very quietly, "You must go home. The police mustn't find you here. Go right away . . . and tell your mama not to worry. You MUST go!"

Nandi felt Khulu push her gently, but firmly, away. Nandi wanted to resist, to stay, but Khulu's face had such a still, sure look that reluctantly she began to move. The white woman was still going on in her high-pitched voice.

"The police won't be long now!"

Themba . . . Zinzi . . . now Khulu! Angry tears blurred out everything as Nandi slipped through the small crowd and ran down to the corner to collect the remaining box of fruit.

Traveling back alone on the train, Nandi thought about Ma. She wondered what Ma had made of her note and whether she had still gone to work. She didn't want to hurt Ma, but Nandi suddenly realized it was no longer a problem what to say, or how to cover up. The typewriter and everything else was now in the open. Searching in her pocket, she pulled out the leaflet from the march—the one she had wanted Esther to hand to Ma. Nandi reread it.

"Parents you should be proud to have children who prefer to die from bullets. . . ."

The police had taken her friends, and now her granny. Her cousin Esther may have escaped, perhaps to carry on fighting . . . Well, she was proud of them! She would tell Ma all about it and give her the leaflet herself.

Eight months later there was a small item in a national newspaper:

GRANDMOTHER SENT TO JAIL

A sixty-eight-year-old grandmother was sent to jail today for twelve months, after refusing to give evidence against two young students charged with sedition and terrorism.

The prosecution said that further charges might

still be laid against Mrs. Miriam Mabale for being in possession of a typewriter alleged to have been used by the accused in the preparation of leaflets calling for the boycott of "apartheid schools," strikes, and armed resistance.

The two accused, Themba Moya and Zinzi Dipale, are alleged to be friends of Mrs. Mabale's granddaughter Esther Mabale who is still being sought by the police.

THE GUN

1985

For years it had been kept carefully secured on a rack above the bed, just beneath the thatch, inside "Boss" Mackay's hut. The long, black barrel pointed toward a prize pair of spiraling kudu horns, fixed to the whitewashed wall along with other trophies from the surrounding bush of Mackay's game farm.

Esi had always been fascinated by the gun's silence and its power. Ever since an early memory of the great lifeless body of a leopard stretched out in the dusty yard—so much bigger than himself. Papa, his father, had been asked to tell the story many times, how during a terrible drought a male leopard had made its way between the huts early one morning, intent upon the enclosure for goats and chickens. Esi's father had managed to rouse Mackay who had grabbed his gun, firing a shot over the animal's head. But instead of bolting away, the creature had rushed at his attacker. The

following shot brought the famished beast crashing, almost at Mackay's feet.

"Such is the desperation of hunger . . ." was how
Papa would always end.

As a little boy, Esi had sat cross-legged on the
leopard-skin mat, gazing up at the gun, while his
father cleaned and polished Mackay's room. When
he was a few years older, and his father's back was
turned, Esi would stand by the bed, quickly
stretching as tall as he could, to run his hand along
the hard metal and smooth wood. He had longed
to be taller, to let his hand explore the gun more
fully. What would it feel like to let his finger curl
gently around the strong metal of the trigger? Of
course he had known that the bolt and bullets were
always removed, locked away separately in a
drawer of the desk.

Now at fifteen, the rack within easy reach, he
had been assigned the task of cleaning the room.
But the gun was no longer above the bed. Ever
since the police had come to warn about "terrorists," Mackay had failed to follow the ritual of
replacing the gun on its rack. Instead, he locked it
in his cupboard.

The square shape and veranda of Mackay's hut (his "bed-sitter in the bush" as he called it to his friends) distinguished it from the other round huts of the camp. It was mostly shut up for weeks at a time while he was away in Jo'burg, always taking the gun with him. A director of a large mining company, he lived in the city, only coming to his game farm at intervals for a break.

"Too much work, too much noise!" he would say to Esi's father.

Sometimes he came for a couple of days, sometimes more. No one knew when he would arrive . . . alone, with his grown-up daughter, or with friends, intending to watch the wildlife from the camouflaged hideout at the water hole, or to track and, when circumstance allowed, to shoot. Nowadays animals were only shot when necessary. As Mackay would tell visitors, his aim was preservation. Indeed wildlife flourished: impalas, zebras, wildebeasts—to name but a few of the herds preyed on by lions, sometimes leopards, with their persistent hangers-on, the hyenas and jackals. Even elephants made their way across the territory from time to time.

It was simply by custom that it was called a

"farm," because apart from the small area in which a few crops were cultivated by Esi's family, it was entirely covered in age-old rough grass; stunted, tangled trees; and bush. Close to the National Game Reserve and adjoining the Hendriks' game farm, it could take you a day to walk across it from one end to the other.

Esi's father looked after the farm when Mackay was away, his main work being to stop poachers. As a child, Esi had found the constant dangers of following Papa through tall grass and rough bush thrilling and exciting. Poachers could be armed, while his father had only his short cutting knife. But Papa could tell so much from noticing a broken twig, a flattened patch of grass, a piece of missing bark, vultures circling. If there was any trouble, he had to notify the white neighbor Hendriks, who would come with his gun and contact the police. Hendriks also made a point of coming over once a week to check all was in order.

However, even when Mackay was there, Esi noticed how his father was able to advise Mackay and answer his questions. Papa knew all about the movement and numbers of animals. If an animal was to be shot, it was Papa who quietly led the

tracking to bring Mackay into the right position
for shooting. It was always Papa who knew if
poachers had set a trap, laying in turn one of his
own. It was Papa who would shout the order for the
poachers to put up their hands. While Mackay or
Hendriks pointed the gun, it was Papa who would
approach the trapped men to remove their belts,
causing their trousers to fall to their ankles. It was
Papa who would interpret for Mackay when the
poachers spoke. Mackay depended almost totally
on Papa. Indeed Esi had once overheard him
saying as much to a visitor:

"You know I couldn't live in the city and run this
place if it wasn't for my boss-boy Isaac."

Yet Papa was never allowed to handle the gun.

Some forty kilometers from the farm was the vil-
lage of Mapoteng, "the place you get to in a round
about way." The land was poor and the people
were poor. Even poorer since the white authorities
had declared Mapoteng part of a "homeland," to
which black people had been sent in their thousands
when their homes were not wanted close to the
towns and cities of whites. Whole families had
found themselves cleared off white-owned farms

and "black spots"; their homes bulldozed to the ground; themselves with their few possessions forced on to great khaki government trucks, the "GGs," and dumped in the dust of Mapoteng—to start life again. Here in this unknown place the government called their "home," they found the earth hard and dry, cracked with overuse and drought. Here they found hunger. In desperation, some sought food in forbidden places.

It was when he was thirteen that Esi had been sent to stay with an aunt in Mapoteng, so he could attend the primary school. There he had begun to learn not only to read but also what it was to eat only a few handfuls of *pap* a day and little else. Although Papa would bring a large bag of mealie meal and some money for his sister (she was looking after another brother's family as well as her own), with ten hungry children in the house, food was often scarce.

In Mapoteng, Esi found people who became silent on hearing who he was. They would look strangely at him, keeping their distance. He soon discovered that there were those who despised his father's job. In fact, it was stronger than that with some. It was hate. To them, his father was simply another detested policeman, protecting the white man's land and a source of food they sorely needed.

At first, Esi had been hurt and confused. Although he had said nothing, he wanted to defend Papa. However as his own stomach learned to know the nagging ache of emptiness, he began to understand something of what people felt. Memories of the childish thrill and excitement of accompanying his father in the bush turned into an inner dread, fed by the troubled thought: *If I had to live always in this place without food, I would also hunt.*

It was not the slow grip of hunger alone, however, that changed Esi. . . .

From time to time news would somehow filter through to Mapoteng about an explosion, a protest, people shot by police. Most of this had seemed very far away to Esi, used to his small world around the camp. However, while others talked, he listened. There were men who lived apart from their families for most of the year, working deep down in the mines near the city. In hoarse voices (as if the dust had stuck in their throats) they spoke of meetings broken up by police with dogs, gas that burned your eyes—and bullets. Some people had been moved from places where there had been boycotts and mass arrests, and where those who disappeared were sometimes rumored to have escaped over the border to join the "MKs." Gradually he gathered that these MKs were people like themselves. But they had resisted the trap of being pushed around and now lived outside the white man's law, prepared to fight to be free of it—even die, to overthrow it. It was plainly a dangerous matter, this fighting for freedom.

Esi's familiar world was overturned finally by the events on one particular day. Without any warning, a line of army trucks had come roaring, hurtling down, dust flying, through the rows of mud and iron huts. Soldiers smashed open doors, wheeling their guns and forcing people outside. The soldier who had barged into his aunty's house had deftly swept her few treasured pieces of crockery off the shelf with his rifle.

Horrified, shocked, they had been herded like cattle to be inspected by the white army chief. But most of the soldiers were black, like themselves. Why were they doing this?

"Don't think you can hide anything from us! If you want to help terrorists you know what you can expect!" the white officer had grimly sneered, his words translated by the black soldier at his side.

As Esi had watched these soldiers shoving and prodding their young suspects with loaded guns, he had felt so angry—and so helpless. They were all so helpless. If only *he* had a gun. . . .

Shortly afterward Esi had become very ill with a fever. Lack of food had made him weak. When his father got word of this, that was the end of schooling for Esi. Papa brought him home, saying there was no point in going to school if it meant starving first. Instead he would begin seriously teaching his son his own work on the game farm.

Esi remembered trying to talk to his father about what was troubling him. But Papa had stopped him short, speaking forcefully. He knew all about the raid on Mapoteng. Police had also visited the farm to tell them about the "terrorists" and how they must report anything unusual. Papa had promised to do so. Esi had to understand that he did his job as "boss-boy" well so that Mackay would depend on him. In return the family got

land, water, food. Indeed they were lucky. Couldn't
Esi see how foolish it was to question this? They
might end up like the people of Mapoteng, with
nothing, and Esi would have to join the queue for
work on the mines.

Papa's voice softened.

"Listen, Esi. . . . This land was taken from our
parents with guns. Those with guns can do what
they please. You had better be very careful before
you say no to a man with a gun. Can you stop a
bullet with bare hands?"

Esi had shaken his head and kept quiet, his
stomach knotted. He couldn't talk to his father,
and he had begun to dread the day when the
poachers would be people he knew. How could he
look them in the eye?

Now, some months later, Mackay was on one of his
visits. Esi was performing his daily chore of collecting and chopping firewood, when Hendriks
drove up in his truck. He seemed agitated, calling
loudly to Esi:

"Waar's die baas?"

Almost before Esi put down the ax, Mackay
appeared from his hut. Hendriks lowered his voice

as he spoke, but Esi could still make out some words. Hendriks was saying something about "ter-rorists" and an "attack on a police station" and "no white man on the farm." Then the two men went inside the hut for a drink.

When they came out again, Hendriks looked more relaxed, and it seemed they had agreed on something. As they shook hands Hendriks said, "Don't worry. He'll have your boss-boy, and I'll give him a hand if he needs it. He'll soon get the hang of the place."

"Well he just hasn't settled to anything since the army. Sometimes you wonder what happens to our boys in there. Those 'terrs' keep them tense, you know. . . ." Mackay paused. "Perhaps this is what he needs . . . sort himself out. I'll get him up here as soon as I can. Thanks for the warning!"

Mackay stood shading his eyes against the sun, watching Hendriks's truck maneuver through the narrow camp gate and bump its way up along the dirt road. When the rumbling had faded away into the bush, Mackay called over to Esi.

"That's enough wood for now, Esi . . . I won't need it tonight. Go and call you father. Tell him I'm leaving very soon."

• • •

Papa didn't say anything until that night when they were eating by the fire and Esi's mother raised the question.

"Why did he go like that?"

She had a way of saying "he" that indicated that she was talking about Mackay.

"He's bringing someone. . . ."

Papa paused and gave a wry, hoarse laugh.

"They want a white in charge . . . to stay. I think it's the one who is going to marry his daughter."

Everyone was silent until Esi's mother clicked.

"That one's mouth is too big."

Esi knew just what his mother meant. When the daughter's boyfriend had visited the farm once before, they were all relieved when he had left, even Papa who never showed his feelings much. At that time the young white man was doing his service in the army and had been on leave. But by now he must have finished his army service.

Esi was wondering whether to intervene in the conversation to report what Hendriks had said about "terrorists," when Papa's cousin spoke. He had cycled over to Mapoteng during the day. Outside the shop he had heard people discussing news of a gun battle between three armed men and police at a place only a hundred kilometers south of Mapoteng. Apparently one man had been killed but two had gotten away. Some youngsters outside the shop had broken into song about MKs. Others, however, were worried there might be another house-to-house search in Mapoteng.

Early the following afternoon, there was the familiar sound of Mackay's Land Rover entering the camp. Esi saw immediately that it was being driven by the young man Williams—and he was alone. When he jumped down from the driver's seat, he was carrying Mackay's gun. Although he could only be a few years older than Esi, there was something in his manner that reminded Esi of the sneering officer in the Mapoteng raid. His bush-green eyes narrowed on their target.

"What're you staring at? You've seen me before, haven't you? Go get your boss-boy for me. Be quick about it, *jong!*"

Esi could feel his face going hot, but he turned rapidly and sprinted off. Even Mackay never spoke to him like that, always calling him by his name.

Esi accompanied his father as he walked forward

to greet the white man. He wanted to see how Papa would react.

"You remember me? . . . Boss Williams. Boss Mackay has asked me to come and look after his place, so we better get on, you and me. I don't want any trouble from the other boys either, OK?" He turned to Esi.

"You can get my bags out the back and carry them to my room." Papa simply gave a slight nod. It was impossible to tell what he was thinking. His lined face remained quite impassive as father and son carried the young white man's cases.

Before long it was apparent that Williams assumed Esi to be his personal servant. Up till now Esi had taken instructions either from his father or Mackay, who had known him since he was little. But this man's manner was different. He didn't seem to care at all who Esi was. It was as if he was just a thing to be used.

Much of the time Williams would sit on the veranda outside Mackay's room, legs stretched out on a stool, a can of beer at his side, while cleaning or fiddling with Mackay's gun.

"Hey, come clean my boots!"

"You can wash the truck now!"

"Make my bed properly, *jong*! Don't just pull the sheets up like that!"

"Do you call these boots clean? If you were in the army I'd donder you! Do them again!"

"Go call the girl! I want her to do my washing this morning."

At the last order, Esi had to fight to control himself. Who did this man think he was? Didn't he know that "the girl" was Esi's own mother, old enough to be the white man's mother? When Esi found her, busy collecting wild spinach, his anger spilled out.

She tried to calm him. His temper would get him into trouble. He should try to be like his father.

"Papa just lets them push him around. I don't want to be like that!"

"Ha! What else can you do my young man?"

And with that his mother began walking slowly, steadily, toward the camp to collect the dirty washing.

It was soon clear that Williams was a heavy drinker. He had brought his personal supply, Papa and Esi having unpacked half a dozen crates of beer and other drink from the Land Rover. On the first night, as Esi passed by in the dark, he had looked into the lit-up sitting room and seen Mackay's special cabinet, usually kept locked, wide open with a half-full bottle of whiskey on the table. Next morning there was an empty bottle in the bin.

Nor was it easy to get to sleep. The heavy silence of the bushveld night usually covered everything like a thick blanket of darkness, except for the customary night sounds—twitchings and chitterings, the odd screech or howl. But now that silence was shattered with a radio blaring out music across the camp into the bush until after midnight.

When Hendriks arrived one afternoon, Williams invited him to have some beer.

"Hell man, I'm glad to see someone! How d'you live in this godforsaken place? I must've been off my head to say yes to the old man!"

The two men sat drinking and smoking on the veranda. Esi stayed out of sight, but within hearing. While he appeared to be polishing the black boots, he was listening intently for any news about the armed guerrillas who had escaped. It seemed they still hadn't been captured and the search was being concentrated further south.

Williams made out to Hendriks that he was patrolling the farm himself. It was a lie. He had only been down to the water hole a couple of

112

OUT OF BOUNDS

times, Mackay's gun slung from his shoulder. Esi and Papa had gone along with him, soon gathering that all Williams really wanted was to shoot a kudu bull, for a prize pair of horns like Mackay's. When Papa had mentioned that this wasn't the season for culling, for once Williams hadn't said anything. But Esi suspected that if a kudu came his way, he'd shoot.

Williams didn't only take over Esi's life. He began to give orders to Papa on the running of the farm. Papa kept quiet at first, fitting in the new instructions with what he normally did.

But the day after Hendriks's visit, when Williams ordered Papa to go to the shop at Mapoteng for cigarettes, Papa replied that he had planned to do a thorough tour of the farm that day. Something in his careful observations had made him uneasy. It would take him over two hours on the old bicycle just to get to Mapoteng. Perhaps the boss would let one of the other workers go? However, Esi heard Williams insist that it should be Papa.

"Don't you think I can manage here on my own?" he rasped.

Esi stopped sweeping the yard. He willed his

father to answer back. Instead, his father, grim faced but silent, slowly mounted the bicycle and rode off.

Esi began sweeping again. He jabbed the broom fiercely at the ground, causing the dust to scatter and fly, the anger he felt spilling out. How did Papa remain calm? Even before this man came, Papa had to play the same game with Mackay. "Boss-boy!" "Boy!" Yet if Mackay never came to the farm, Papa could still keep it running. Still, Mackay wasn't vicious like the man his daughter wanted to marry. What would happen if they did get married? Would Williams take over the farm? But whoever owned the place, Esi didn't want to be their policeman. Dust swirling up and around, he began to feel despair choking him.

"What the hell do you think you're doing? Can't you sweep properly? Hurry up with that job. I want you to come with me."

With the gun slung at his side, and binoculars hanging around his neck, Williams set off through the bush, followed by Esi.

There were no animals at the water hole. In the heat of the day, they would take to whatever shade they could find, coming for water only when the sun was going down. Williams thrust forward on his way to the other side of the water and began to follow a track through long dry grass and thorn trees up a low slope. With his father, Esi usually felt confident, Papa would move very quietly, always alert against possible danger. He could trust Papa's reactions despite his being unarmed.

Now, however, Esi felt nervous. Williams was too much on edge. At a sudden movement in the nearby bush, Esi froze. Williams whirled around, swinging the gun forward. But before he could locate his target, Esi had already looked into the wide eyes of a terrified little steenbuck, flickering past him through the tall grass. The gun was almost pointing at Esi before Williams lowered it, grunting a curse. This man was mad. Esi decided to lag as far behind him as possible.

As they moved further and further from the water hole, Esi wondered whether Williams could find his way back. He was probably expecting to get his bearings from the top of the low hill since most of the land around was fairly flat.

Once at the top, Williams walked to the edge of the ridge overlooking the other side. He scanned the veld below for a few minutes with his binoculars.

"*Ja!* There he is! What a beaut!"

Esi followed the direction of the binoculars. His eyes trailed along a dry riverbed, searching the bush on its banks. Suddenly a slight movement defined the subtle curves of a gray kudu bull, its horns like converging branches. Lowering the binoculars, Williams signaled the way.

It was while they were still descending the ridge that Esi noticed what looked like a cave. There was no time to investigate. However, he also observed that the grass seemed flattened in a patch around the cave. Looking back for a second or two, he steadied himself by lightly touching the branch of a tree. As he lifted his hand off the branch, careful to avoid the thorns, a piece of brown thread caught his eye. It was wool, as though a piece from someone's clothing had caught on the thorn. Whose was it? At that point Williams turned and whispered fiercely, "Hurry up, *jong*! I'll donder you if you make me lose him."

Esi's mind was now racing as he struggled to keep pace with Williams. Poachers wouldn't need a cave. They would come and go as quickly as possible, simply to set and collect from their traps. Their safety lay in merging back into Mapoteng. Maybe someone else had been hiding here. Esi could feel his heart pumping rapidly as he recalled the conversation on the veranda. The MKs still hadn't been captured. If he was Papa, he would contact Hendriks right away so the matter could be reported.

Williams turned around again.

"Come on, you. . . ."

Before he could finish, he had tripped over an out-stretched tree root. A sharp, ear-splitting crack lashed the air, followed by a howl of pain. Williams' body lurched forward and struck the ground, the gun hurtling away on impact. When Esi reached him, he was squirming in the rough tall grass, clutching the leg he had shot.

"God, *jong*! . . . The safety catch came undone! . . . Help me tie something around . . ."

Esi held back, watching as Williams struggled to tear off his shirt and tightly bandage his lower leg. The pain showed on his face.

"What're you waiting for? Help me up, *jong*!"

Still Esi hesitated, caught by an angry desire to laugh out loud at the helplessness of this man normally so high and mighty. Shot by his own gun—or Mackay's gun, what did it matter! When Esi did kneel down, Williams saw, perhaps for the first time, the contempt in the young man's eyes.

"You're strong enough to help me, damn it, aren't you?"

But as Williams began to put his weight on Esi in levering himself up, Esi suddenly let himself go limp. . . .

No. He was not going to help this man.

Williams bellowed and swore at Esi personally and "the whole bloody lot of you." The curses seemed to hang above them, echoing in the hot, otherwise silent bushveld air. Esi could see a dangerous look in Williams's eyes, as if the white man would have liked to crush him, injure him in some way too. He began to struggle to get away, but Williams was clutching him, forcing him down. With the white man's powerful hand edging toward his throat, Esi managed to free one leg, kick Williams on his wound, and wriggle free as a fearful scream rang in his ears.

Esi was shaking as he got to his feet. He saw the gun lying on the ground and almost without thinking picked it up and began to stumble back toward the ridge. His last image was of Williams trying to force himself up, groaning and cursing, with blood seeping through the makeshift bandage.

His mind was in turmoil. He couldn't go back to

the camp now. When it was found out what he had done, he would be arrested, surely beaten up and sentenced to years in jail. He'd heard plenty about jail in Mapoteng. In the white court all the sympathy would be for Williams. And if the man by any chance died? . . . Esi's mind blanked out. He didn't even know why he had taken the gun.

It had all happened so quickly. It seemed he had always been trapped and now he could quite easily be destroyed. Williams was like the soldiers who smashed up his aunty's house. He thought he had a right to push Esi around, while Esi had no right to disobey. Yes, Esi hated him and his power that ensnared all their lives. He didn't want to be like Papa, powerless, accepting the trap just so they could all keep on living—in the trap. Even maintaining the trap by catching poachers, black people like themselves, only starving. "Such is the desperation of hunger. . . ." He could hear Papa's own voice at the end of the leopard story. But how could you ever escape?

Esi came to the bottom of the ridge. He flopped down to rest against a boulder in a stony gulley, his head in his hands, Mackay's gun at his side. He must stop and think. He was going in the wrong direction, back towards the camp. Ah! He'd forgotten about the cave. What if those two MKs had been there, were there? Surely they were trying to escape the trap. They had arms. Arms against arms. At least they had a chance. . . . So why shouldn't he have the gun? In Mapoteng he'd heard songs about young people going for "training" outside the country. Somehow they found their way across the border. From here it was to the east. What was it like? The high barbed-wire fence around the police station in Mapoteng? What about guards? Police and soldiers would surely be like flies on meat in the area near the border. He would have to travel by night. . . .

Sitting alone in the gulley at the bottom of the ridge, Esi slowly realized that he had made his choice. He had made it at the moment he had let his body go limp, refusing to support Williams. There was no going back now. If only he could say good-bye to his family . . . hug them, especially his mother . . . for a last time try and explain to Papa. But it could not be. He would simply climb up to the cave . . . find out what was there . . . perhaps have a sleep . . . and at night, set out cast, with the gun.

THE PLAYGROUND

1995

The word "dead!" struck Rosa as she drew near the cluster of children on the other side of the fence. She looked up and saw a boy pointing his fore-finger at her through the criss-cross wire fence. He pulled his finger back sharply while his cheeks and lips exploded a short pistol blast. For a second she hesitated, her heart racing. She wanted to run. But that's what they were waiting for. Instead she forced herself to glance at all their faces. The narrow knife-gray eyes of Trigger-boy glinted with spite from under his corn-tassel fringe. But the others were more curious. Like cats hoping to play with a mouse.

Trigger-boy screwed up his mouth, preparing some new missile. Rosa pressed her lips tightly. She made herself walk steadily on, shifting her gaze into the playground behind the fence. Why shouldn't she look inside if she chose? But with the children's laughter now breaking behind her, she felt hot and angry. They seemed about her own age. Eleven . . . some even younger. And it was to their school that Mama wanted her to go after Christmas! She and Mama had read the words of the white head teacher in the newspaper. He didn't like the new law from the new government. Too bad, said Mama. He would have to obey it. When the new school year began in January, he must open the doors of his school. Mama wasn't prepared to wait a day longer for her own daughter to be admitted.

The playground was alive with chasing, skipping, running, shouting. A few children sat quietly on benches in the shade of lacy jacarandas that formed a boundary of pale-green giant umbrellas between the tarmac and the playing fields. The well-kept grass stretched from the main road as far as a line of distant blue gums. They were the same tall gray trees that Rosa saw as she crossed the rough dry veld separating the township where she and Mama lived from what she had always known as the white people's town.

It was lunch break at Oranje Primary School. Inside the grand double-storied, orange-brick building with its neat rows of sparkling windows, children had classes both morning and afternoon. Not like in her school. *Her* school in the township had so many pupils they had to take turns to use the classrooms! When she and her classmates finished lessons at twelve, the afternoon children were just arriving. There was no playground to talk of, just a stretch of dry ground and a few straggly cactus plants in front of a long row of single-story classrooms.

Rosa eyed a group of girls around a net-ball post, one poised on her toes with upstretched arm taking aim. Normally she would have stopped or slowed down to watch. Or she would spend a little time looking out for Hennie. Usually she only had to check through the boys chasing after a ball. It was a little game that she still played, seeing if she could spot him. Of course, he never saw her. Or if he did, he never let on.

"*Dumela,* sis!"

The boy who sold newspapers to passing motorists at the corner lights called out to Rosa as she approached. His dark eyes, set deep in a pinched nut-brown face, seemed concerned. Had he seen? The road was quiet, and he was standing next to his stack of papers in a faded blue T-shirt pitted with holes.

"Dumela!" Rosa tried to smile before turning the corner.

She broke into a jog. She could no longer be seen by Trigger-boy's gang from here, and she wanted to get away as quickly as possible. On her left, iron railings with slim black spearheads protected the stern archway entrance to Oranje Primary School. Even the yellow roses were forbidding, standing like soldiers in straight lines.

Rosa didn't want to be late. Hennie's mother might deduct something from the few rands she was paying her to look after the twins.

When Mevrou van Niekerk had asked Mama some months ago if Rosa could help for a few hours every day after she finished morning school, Rosa had been upset. She never wanted to go back there! She had never forgotten Hennie's father and the words he had said all those years ago. But Mama had pointed out they would need every cent in the New Year. President Mandela's new law might say that all government schools would be open to every child, but Mama knew the people of Oranje.

"They'll tell us there's this fund and that fund. But we'll be ready. They're not going to keep their

Oranje Primary School just for their Hennies. It's going to be for my Rosa too!"

Only a few months earlier, for the first time in her life, Mama had stood in the same long winding queue as Hennie's parents and the other white townfolk, waiting to cast her vote for their new government. A "rainbow government," Mama told Rosa. A government that would make sure her daughter could attend a school with enough classrooms, teachers, desks, books, and playing fields for everyone. The school that the white parents had kept just for their own children would have to become a "rainbow school." Mama had laughed.

At first Rosa had felt excited. She and her friends talked about what it would be like to go to a school that had been "whites only." But the nearer it got to the end of term and the start of the new school year, the more Rosa began to worry. Parents in the township were beginning to change their minds about sending their children to Oranje Primary after Christmas. Her best friend Thato's parents wanted to "wait and see." Maybe the new government would send extra teachers to their own school. Maybe there would be money to build new classrooms and buy books.

There were rumors of trouble. Someone's father had overheard talk of a "White School Defense Committee." Nearly every white home in Oranje had at least one gun locked in a safe. Rosa herself had seen burly red-faced men in town with pistols strapped to their belts. Often they dressed from head to foot in khaki. With their wide-brimmed khaki hats they appeared like characters from old war films. Mama had told her to keep well out of their way. Rosa hardly needed the warning. She had never seen Hennic's father, Meneer van Niekerk, with a gun, but she had a vivid imagination.

Mama had worked for Mevrou van Niekerk for years, and Rosa had known Hennie since they were babies. At three they had played together. Mama used to take her every weekday. While Mama cooked, cleaned, washed, and ironed, Rosa and Hennie had scampered around the garden, built castles in the sandpit, made houses in the dry donga at the end of the long garden where the bushes grew wild.

By the time Rosa and Hennie were five, Mevrou van Niekerk no longer worried if Hennie was out of her sight for an hour or two. They always came

back as soon as they were hungry, and Mama
would pour them both milk and give them cakes or
scones, whatever she had freshly baked. Hennie
was now a big brother, and Mevrou van Niekerk
was largely kept busy with her twin babies.

Usually Meneer van Niekerk left home early,
before Mama and Rosa had arrived, and returned
after they had left. Mama never took Rosa with her
on Saturdays and Sundays. When Rosa was old
enough to ask why, Mama had explained that
Hennie's father "liked quiet." Rosa told Mama that
she and Hennie could be very quiet. They could
play all day in the donga. Mama had said that
Hennie's father wouldn't like that. The few times
Rosa had seen him, he had never smiled. Rosa
decided she would not like to see him angry.
Hennie had told her about his father's belt. How
he had beaten him with it one evening after trip-
ping over a rope the children had tied between two
paw-paw trees to practice jumping.

"I didn't tell on you," Hennie had told her,
showing her the marks on the back of his legs with
some pride. "And Ma didn't tell him!"

"What would your daddy do to me?" Rosa had
asked.

Hennie had answered by sharply sucking in his breath as he pulled back his lips to show his teeth. Rosa felt her skin tingle as they began to collect dry grass to make a roof for the new house they were making.

Their playing together had come to a sudden end when one day Meneer van Niekerk came home early. The two of them were dashing under the sprinkler, shrieking and pulling funny faces for the twins, who were sitting up in their pram and gurgling, when Hennie's father strode across the lawn. Like a thunderstorm he swept Hennie up with one arm and began to smack him on the bottom with the flat of his other hand. Hennie's cries of laughter turned to cries of pain.

"*Wat makeer jy?* What do you think you're doing? Running around like a savage? Half-naked with this *piccanin?*"

The words had slapped Rosa too. Mevrou van Niekerk and Mama had both come running from the house.

"Is this how you're letting him grow? It's time he learnt to be a proper boy—and to know he's a *white* boy!"

Rosa saw Mama's shoulders rise ever so slightly.

Mama had taken Rosa silently by the hand and led her away. Above Hennie's sobs and the babies' cries, she heard Mevrou van Niekerk.

"They were just playing, Willem. Just children's games. Look how you've frightened them."

After that, Mama had left Rosa every day with their neighbor, Mrs. Moloi. She was a kind old lady who looked after a couple of younger children as well. Rosa liked them but missed her games with Hennie. It would not be long, said Mama, before Rosa would start at the nearby school and have lots of friends of her own age to play with. But when the new year came and Mama took Rosa, in the maroon school pinafore that had been her Christmas present, they were turned away from the township school. The head teacher had explained that there were already eighty six-year-olds in a room meant for forty. He took their names and said he was sorry but they would have to wait another year. So Rosa returned to Mrs. Moloi. Mama let her wear her school uniform. She was growing quickly and it would be wasted otherwise.

Rosa had asked Mama about Hennie.

"Is Hennie waiting to go to school, Mama?"

Mama did not answer at first, but when Rosa

asked again, she replied briefly, "No. He started at Oranje Primary."

But only three weeks after Rosa had been turned away from the overcrowded school, a spirit of joy blossomed like an unexpected rainbow for a few days over the entire township. Neighbors and friends had crowded into their tiny sitting room, while Rosa sat wedged on Mama's lap, watching a tall silver-haired man with a warm, serious but smiling face wave at them from their small television set. All around Rosa people were crying and laughing.

Unbelievable, they said. It was a day they had almost thought would never come. Nelson Mandela, the man the white government had locked up for life, was walking free from his prison! Here was their Madiba coming to help them. They prayed for him to chase away the heavy gray clouds thrown over their lives by the white people's government.

When Rosa had returned to the van Niekerks' house to look after the twins, six years after Hennie's father had chased her away, she had dreaded seeing him again. But as Mama had

predicted, now that Rosa was just a *kleinmeid* working in the house, Meneer van Niekerk hardly
noticed her. With Hennie too, she sometimes felt
quite invisible.

The first time he had come home from school
and seen her in the kitchen, there was a brief
moment when he had seemed curious. He had
even nodded a greeting. But after that he always
appeared to be occupied or on his way somewhere.

At the start of the Christmas holidays, Hennie's
mother asked Rosa to help all day including
Saturdays. So Rosa accompanied Mama early each
morning and returned home with her in the
evenings, quite exhausted. Even so, she earned
only a few rands more each week for all the extra
hours.

"It must be nice for you to be with your mother
all day and earn some pocket money!" Mevrou van
Niekerk commented one time, when handing Rosa
her money. "I wish I could see as much of
Hennie!"

Hennie, it seemed, spent most of his time playing rugby. Mama was forever scrubbing clothes
covered in red dirt.

"He'll be our first Springbok in the family!"

Mevrou van Niekerk said proudly to some
Saturday visitors. Hennie looked a little embarrassed.

"That's if the blacks haven't taken all the places
by then," Meneer van Nickerk spoke as if he were
tasting a lemon.

Hennie glanced at his father but did not say
anything.

Another time, Rosa overheard Mevrou van
Niekerk speaking to Mama in the kitchen about
"this silly trouble at the school."

"It's good for the new government to help
people. But I don't know why they must force children together in such a hurry!"

Mama's knife continued chopping at the same
steady pace. She said nothing. Rosa marveled at
how she could cover up.

All through the school holidays while working
with Mama at the van Niekerks, Rosa kept hoping
that Thato's parents would let her start at Oranje
Primary too. But one evening as they passed
the paperboy, she read the headlines: "WHITE
PARENTS TO PROTEST." Mama stopped to buy
a copy.

"Do you know that President Mandela wants

every child to be in school?" Mama asked as she handed over the coins. "When will your mother send you to school?"

"My mother is dead," the boy said gravely. "If I go to school, I won't have money for food."

A car hooted and he darted away to sell another paper.

One night, just after Christmas, Rosa was rinsing the dishes under the tap in the yard, when Mama called her.

"You can finish that later! Come and watch."

Mama patted the cushion next to her on the small sofa. Rosa curled up close. On the television an interviewer was asking children what it was like to go to a school that used to be only for white children.

"At first I was scared," said a boy with a stylish haircut. "Ree-aally scared."

He paused, biting his lower lip. The other children laughed nervously.

"I thought no one would be my friend. But now I have lots of friends," he added with a broad smile.

"It was like that for me too," said a girl with a serious bronze face and thick long black hair. "You think no one will like you and they're probably thinking the same."

"Indian children go to that school too, Mama," Rosa nudged Mama.

"And *we* were wondering what *you* would be like!" giggled a freckled, pink-cheeked girl with a mass of blond curls. "You know how people pass round stories."

"Especially horror ones!" interrupted the stylish-haired boy.

"You see," said Mama, during the advertisements. "It won't be so bad, will it, Rosa?"

"But, Mama, those white children aren't like the ones at Oranje Primary."

"My grandmother taught me an old Zulu saying: *Ubuntu ungumuntu ngabanye abantu. . . .* People are people through other people. It means we are who we are in the way we treat others. Even here, Rosa, people will begin to learn that too."

The reporter was back, talking about schools that still took only white children. A boy with a missing front tooth stared cheekily at the camera.

"Soon your school won't be allowed to turn away black children, Andries. Do you look forward to making new friends?"

"There won't be any of them after eleven."
Andries grinned.

"Why is that?"

"It won't be nice for them at break."

"What are you going to do?" the reporter asked
calmly.

The boy's grin widened as he shrugged his
shoulders. Rosa chewed her thumb.

"That's what they're like here," she whispered
under her breath.

Mama heard. She pulled her closer and hugged
her. "Not all of them, Rosa . . . and someone has to
go first."

New Year arrived and soon afterward it was the day
that Rosa had begun to dread. Walking down their
road for the first time in her new Oranje Primary
uniform, she felt everyone was staring at her and
Mama. Old Mrs. Moloi wiped her eyes and called
out good luck over the wall. But a group of older
boys, sitting on crates outside the supermarket,
stopped chatting as they passed. She thought she
heard one of them say "whitey." Mama took her
hand.

"Don't let anyone take who you are away from

you, my child," she said gently but firmly.

As they crossed the veld and entered the town, Mama's hand gave Rosa small squeezes of encouragement. Before they had even reached the corner of Oranje Primary, they could see a crowd of adults and children, lined up by the front entrance. It seemed like Trigger-boy's gang had grown taller and bigger, a hundred times over. A small gathering of policemen stood a short distance away, next to a man and a woman wearing suits and each carrying a briefcase. The crowd by the gate were all white but some of the police were black, as was the man in the dark suit. Everyone appeared to be waiting for something, including the paperboy. He stood at the corner watching Rosa and Mama approach. He looked worried.

Mama squeezed her hand more tightly as they reached the protesters. Faces and placards became blurred, but Rosa couldn't blot out the hoarse screams: "NEVER! WHITE AND BLACK DON'T MIX!" "FIGHT FOR A WHITE ORANJE!" "NO BLACKS HERE."

Mama never turned her face. Rosa, however, took a quick peek behind her and saw that the man and lady with briefcases were following. At the top of the steps, under the entrance arch, stood a stern, grim man. His folded cheeks were shades of gray and his eyes, behind the thick glasses, reminded Rosa of a rhino standing guard. Was this the head teacher? She felt her stomach twist. A man with a deep-red face under a large khaki hat was arguing with him from the bottom of the steps. He jabbed his finger in Rosa's direction.

"If you let this one in, we'll take all our children away! I'm warning you!" He stretched out his arms to stop Rosa and Mama going up.

"If I don't let her in, the government will close the school! Don't you understand?" The head teacher sounded like he was pleading. Then he glared toward the couple with briefcases. "We have no choice!" he said bitterly.

Rosa heard a clicking sound. A camera loomed toward her, clicking again.

"This has echoes of Little Rock!" A man with an American accent was speaking into a microphone. "What's it like to come to a school where people don't want you?"

He thrust the microphone near her mouth.

"They will want me when they know me!" Rosa replied softly but clearly. But before he could ask anything more, the man in the khaki hat started to push him violently away. The policemen rushed forward and the next thing Rosa knew was that she and Mama were somehow at the top of the steps, being hurried by the grim-faced head teacher into an office.

The forms filled in, Mama had to leave. She would have to face the protesters again and explain to Mevrou van Niekerk why she was late. Rosa tried not to feel panic as she watched Mama go. She followed the head teacher in the opposite direction down a long corridor and up the stairs to the Standard Three classroom.

As soon as she entered the doorway, she saw him—Trigger-boy. He sat in the far corner of the room, gazing straight at her. Why couldn't he be one of the children whose parents took them away? Why did he have to be in her class? The teacher pointed to an empty place by the window, two desks in front of Trigger-boy. Rosa saw everyone's eyes turn from her to the girl who would be sitting next to her. She struggled to remain calm as she walked across the room.

"Eyes on your work, class. I expect at least two pages by break." The teacher's crisp voice was followed by a warning from the head teacher. He was still standing by the door.

"I expect no nonsense too! I want to hear no bad reports from Miss Brink."

"*Ja*, Meneer Botha!" the class chorused.

Rosa heard a low snigger behind her as the head teacher left. Miss Brink looked young but severe. Her lips were a deeper red than her rust-colored hair, which was pulled tightly back into a neat bun. She walked briskly down the aisle to Rosa with an exercise book.

"The title for your composition is on the board. Let's see how good your English is."

Rosa stared at the two words "My Holidays." She hadn't really had a holiday. Did she want to tell Miss Brink that she had been working as a *klein-meid* at Hennie van Niekerk's house? She was wondering whether she should make something up, when she heard Miss Brink talking to her.

"There's no time to sit around. I expect you to catch up with the others."

The girl in the desk next to her caught Rosa's eye and made a quick "better watch out!" face. It wasn't unfriendly. Carefully writing her name and "Standard Three Oranje Primary School" on her new English book, Rosa remembered Mama's words: "Don't let anyone take away from you who you are."

Well, she would tell Miss Brink how she had spent her holidays. Although Hennie was in the class above, he would probably tell his friends and word would spread anyway. And it was nothing to be ashamed of. Rosa smoothed down the first page and began to write.

As soon as she started on the mischief that the twins got up to, there was no stopping. Only once she paused briefly, peering out of the window past the lacy tops of the jacarandas and down to the playground. How strange to see it from this side of the fence! But she wasn't looking forward to going out there at all. If only Thato was with her. She returned to her writing. It took her mind off the coming breaktime and when the bell rang, she had reached the end of her second page. Miss Brink asked if someone would like to take "our new girl" out to play. The girl next to Rosa volunteered.

"Thank you, Marie," said Miss Brink. "And show her where to find the toilets."

Rosa kept her eyes on Marie's mouse-colored plaits as they tramped with the crowd down the stairs. Yet again Rosa was aware of sideways glances. They had just reached a corridor leading towards the playground, when someone tapped her on the shoulder.

"Meneer Botha wants to see you," a girl panted. "Don't worry, Marie, I'll take her."

Rosa looked from the girl to Marie. Why was she being sent for? She was anxious but didn't want to show it.

"Come," said the girl when Marie had left. "We'll go to the office this way."

The girl began to lead her in the opposite direction to everyone else, along a corridor with Standard Four and Five classrooms. It was after they turned into a narrow alley leading out into a deserted yard, however, that Rosa became really worried. On one side was a windowless wall with a wooden door and two large metal bins. In the distance the playing fields stretched out, still and silent.

"But the office, isn't it near the entrance?" Rosa's pulse beat faster, as if sensing an invisible trap.

"*Ja,* it is. I'm just showing you round our school."

The girl's voice was calm, except there was a

slight stress on the "our." Faint sounds of children's laughter and shouts came from the playground on the other side of the building.

They were halfway across the yard when Trigger-boy and a small posse of children stepped out in front of them from behind the bins. His elbows swaggered outward, hands resting on hips.

"You!" he demanded. "Come here!"

Rosa stood rooted to the spot, the knife-gray eyes burrowing into her. She was aware of the girl at her side shifting slightly, as if ready to grab her should she try to run back. Folding her arms, she clutched her sides. She hoped they couldn't tell that she was shaking inside as she stared back squarely.

"My name is Rosa."

Trigger-boy wrinkled back his upper lip, showing his front teeth. Like a bulldog. "What did you say?" he drawled.

She knew he had heard. Her lips sealed themselves, and her mind raced desperately as five sets of eyes pinned her down. This time there was no fence between them.

"Anyone seen a rose this color?" he sneered to the others.

"Yuk!"

"Do you think we can pick her?"

Trigger-boy snapped his fingers. His hand whirled like a crazy wasp. Rosa clenched her fists. She would fight them if she had to.

"Leave Rosa alone!"

She knew that voice! Swinging around, she saw Hennie stride out of the alley. His angry eyes and forehead were so like his father's! Even his voice had the same fierceness. Rosa's stomach did a somersault.

"*Ag*, Hennie, we're only playing," whined the girl who had led Rosa out to the yard.

Hennie ignored her. Trigger-boy and his friends were suddenly deflated, like let-down balloons. Hennie turned to Rosa.

"The playground is that side. I'll show you."

Before they were out of earshot, Rosa heard Trigger-boy complaining loudly.

"Just because he's in Standard Four and good at rugby, he thinks he can boss us around."

Hennie took no notice.

"I saw you and your ma come to school this morning . . . with all those people." He paused awkwardly. "You were very brave."

They turned the corner, following a path along-side the orange-brick building. Hennie walked a little more slowly. Rosa's heart was still thumping. She let Hennie's words sink in. Did they mean that Hennie didn't like the protesters? But surely his father thought like them! They were coming to the playground. Already Rosa could see children on the tarmac ahead glancing in their direction. She stopped and turned to Hennie.

"Somebody has to be first," she said.

Before he could reply, there was a shout. "*Ag*, Hennie, we're waiting for you! Hurry up, man!"

"I've got to go, OK?" Hennie's voice was low.

"Thank you, Hennie," she said simply, pausing slightly before saying his name.

His face flushed a little, then he disappeared into a cluster of boys tumbling after a ball.

Rosa scanned the playground. She deliberately took no notice of the stares. Her eyes traveled across the tarmac, and beyond the children who were chasing, skipping, running, and shouting, to the criss-cross wire fence. In the distance, she glimpsed the paperboy slipping in between cars at the red light. On the way home she would ask him if something was in the paper. A broken placard rested lopsided against the wire. "NEVER! WHITE AND BLA . . ." If the protesters came again, she would have to learn to face them on her own. Mama couldn't come with her every morning and be late for work.

But that was tomorrow. Rosa gave her head a little shake. One step at a time, as Mama would say. Her eyes reached the benches under the jacarandas. A girl with mouse-colored plaits seemed to be looking in her direction. It was Marie. Was she smiling? It was hard to make out from this far. Rosa took a deep breath and stepped out on to the tarmac to cross the playground.

OUT OF BOUNDS

2 0 0 0

Out of bounds.

That's what his parents said as soon as the squatters took over the land below their house. Rohan's dad added another meter of thick concrete bricks to their garden wall and topped it with curling barbed wire. He certainly wasn't going to wait for the first break-in and be sorry later. They lived on the ridge of a steep hill with the garden sloping down. Despite the high wall, from his bedroom upstairs, Rohan could see over the spiked-wire circles down to the place where he and his friends used to play. The wild fig trees under which they had made their hideouts were still there. They had spent hours dragging planks, pipes, sheets of metal and plastic—whatever might be useful—up the hill from rubbish tipped in a ditch below. The first squatters pulled their hideouts apart and used the same old scraps again for their own constructions. Rohan could still see the "ski slope"—the

red earth down which he and his friends had
bumped and flown on a couple of old garbage can
lids. The squatters used it as their road up the hill.
Now it looked like a crimson scar cut between the
shacks littering the hillside.

"There's only one good thing about this busi-
ness," Ma said after the back wall was completed.
"We won't have to wash that disgusting red dust
out of your clothes any more!"

Rohan said nothing. How could he explain what
he had lost?

At first, some of the squatter women and children
came up to the houses with buckets asking for water.
For a couple of weeks his mother opened the gate
after checking that no men were hanging around in
the background. She allowed the women to fill their
buckets at the outside tap. Most of her neighbors
found themselves doing the same. Torrential rains
and floods had ushered in the new millennium by
sweeping away homes, animals and people in the
north of the country. The television was awash with
pictures of homeless families and efforts to help
them. No one knew from where exactly the squatters had come. But, as Ma said, how could you
refuse a woman or child some water?

It wasn't long before all that changed. The first complaint of clothes disappearing off the washing line came from their new neighbors. The first African family, in fact, to move in among the Indians on Mount View. No one had actually seen anyone but everyone was suspicious including the neighbor, Mrs. Zuma.

"You can't really trust these people, you know," Mrs. Zuma tutted when she came to ask if Ma had seen anyone hanging around. However, it was when thieves broke into old Mrs. Pillay's house, grabbed the gold thali from around her neck, and left her with a heart attack that views hardened. Young men could be seen hanging around the shacks. Were some of them not part of the same gang? Mrs. Pillay's son demanded the police search through the settlement immediately. But the police argued they would need more evidence and that the thieves could have come from anywhere.

A new nervousness now gripped the house owners on top of the hill. Every report of theft, break-in, or car hijacking, anywhere in the country, led to another conversation about the squatters on the other side of their garden walls.

At night Rohan peered through the bars of his window before going to sleep. Flickering lights from candles and lamps were the only sign that people were living out there in the thick darkness. In the daytime, when Ma heard the bell and saw that it was a woman or child with a bucket, she no longer answered the call.

All the neighbors were agreed. Why should private house owners be expected to provide water for these people? That was the Council's job. If the squatters were refused water, then perhaps they would find somewhere else to put up their shacks. A more suitable place. Or even, go back to where they came from.

The squatters did not go away. No one knew from where they managed to get their water or how far they had to walk. On the way to school, Rohan and his dad drove past women walking with buckets on their heads.

"These people are tough as ticks! You let them settle and it's impossible to get them out," complained Dad. "Next thing they'll be wanting our electricity."

But Rohan wasn't really listening. He was

scanning the line of African children who strag-
gled behind the women and who wore the black
and white uniform of Mount View Primary, his old
school. He had been a pupil there until his parents
had moved him to his private school in Durban
with its smaller classes, cricket pitch, and its own
rugby ground. Most of the African children at
Mount View had mothers who cleaned, washed,
and ironed for the families on top of the hill. But
since the New Year they had been joined by the
squatter children and each week the line grew
longer.

The queue of traffic at the crossroads slowed
them down, giving Rohan more time to find the
"wire car" boy. He was looking for a boy who
always steered a wire car in front of him with a long
handle. He was about his own age—twelve or thirteen perhaps—and very thin and wiry himself.
What interested Rohan was that the boy never had
the same car for more than two or three days. Nor
had he ever seen so many elaborate designs simply
made out of wire, each suggesting a different make
of car. They were much more complicated than the
little wire toys in the African Crafts shop at the
mall.

"Hey, cool!" Rohan whistled. "See that, Dad?" The boy must have heard because he glanced toward them. His gaze slid across the silver hood of their car toward the trunk but didn't rise up to look at Rohan directly.

"It's a Merc—like ours, Dad! What a beaut! Do you think—"

"*Don't* think about it, son! You want us to stop and ask how much he wants, don't you?"

Rohan half frowned, half smiled. How easily his father knew him!

"No way! If we start buying from these people, we'll be encouraging them! That's not the message we want them to get now, is it?"

Rohan was quiet. He couldn't argue with his dad's logic. If the squatters moved away, he and his friends could get their territory back again.

Rohan returned home early from school. A precious half day. In the past he would have spent it in his hideout. Instead he flicked on the television. News. As his finger hovered over the button to switch channels, the whirr of a helicopter invaded the living room.

"Hey, Ma! Look at this!"

Ma appeared from the kitchen, her hands cupped, white and dusty with flour. On the screen, a tight human knot swung at the end of a rope above a valley swirling with muddy water.

"A South African Air Force rescue team today saved a baby from certain death just an hour after she was born in a tree. Her mother was perched in the tree over floodwaters that have devastated Mozambique. The mother and her baby daughter were among the lucky few. Many thousands of Mozambicans are still waiting to be lifted to safety from branches and rooftops. They have now been marooned for days by the rising water that has swallowed whole towns and villages."

"Those poor people! What a place to give birth!" Ma's floury hands almost looked ready to cradle a baby.

Rohan was watching how the gale from the rotors forced the leaves and branches of the tree to open like a giant flower until the helicopter began to lift. Members of the mother's family still clung desperately to the main trunk. Rohan saw both fear and determination in their eyes.

He and Ma listened to the weather report that followed. Although Cyclone Eline was over,

Cyclone Gloria was now whipping up storms across the Indian Ocean and heading toward Mozambique. Where would it go next? Durban was only down the coast. Rohan had seen a program about a sect who believed the new millennium would mark the end of the world. They were convinced that the floods were a sign that The End was beginning.

"What if the cyclone comes here, Ma?"

"No, we'll be all right son. But that lot out there will get it. The government really should do something." Ma nodded in the direction of the squatters.

"Now, let me finish these *rotis* for your sister!"

Ma returned to her bread making. When she had finished, she wanted Rohan to come with her to his married sister's house. He pleaded to stay behind.

"I've got homework to do Ma! I'll be fine."

"You won't answer the door unless it's someone we know, will you?"

"No Ma!" he chanted. Ma said the same thing every time.

Alone in the house, Rohan daydreamed at his

desk. He was close enough to the window to see down the hill. What if there was so much rain that a river formed along the road below! As the water rose, people would have to abandon their shacks to climb higher up. They would be trapped between the flood below and the torrents above. In assembly they had heard the story of Noah building the ark. Perhaps it wasn't just a story after all. Perhaps the people had tried to cling on to the tops of trees as tightly as those they had seen on television.

Tough as ticks.

The phrase popped into his mind. Wasn't that what his dad had said about the squatters? Yet the one sure way to get rid of ticks was to cover them in liquid paraffin. Drown them. A terrible thought. He should push it right away.

Rohan was about to stretch out for his math book when a figure caught his eye on the old ski slope. It was the thin wiry boy, but he wasn't pushing a car this time. He was carrying two large buckets, one on his head, the other by his side. He descended briskly down the slope and turned along the road in the opposite direction to that taken by the women who carried buckets on their heads. Rohan followed the figure until he went out of sight, then forced himself to open his book.

The bell rang just as he was getting interested in the first question. Nuisance! He hurried to the landing. If someone was standing right in front of the gate, it was possible to see who it was from the window above the stairs. He stood back, careful not to be seen himself. It was the same boy, an empty container on the ground each side of him! Didn't he know not to come to the house up here? But he was only a child, and it looked as if he just wanted some water. It would be different if it were an adult or a complete stranger. Rohan's daydream also made him feel a little guilty. He could see the boy look anxiously through the bars, his hand raised as if wondering whether to ring the bell again. Usually when the boy was pushing his wire car on the way to school, he appeared relaxed and calm.

By the time the bell rang a second time, Rohan had decided. He hurried downstairs but slowed himself as he walked outside toward the gate.

"What do you want?" Rohan tried not to show that he recognized the boy.

"I need water for my mother. Please." The boy held his palms out in front of him as if asking for a favor. "My mother—she's having a baby—it's bad—there's no more water. Please."

This was an emergency. Not on television but right in front of him. Still Rohan hesitated. His parents would be extremely cross that he had put himself in this situation by coming to talk to the boy. Weren't there stories of adults who used children as decoys to get people to open their gates so they could storm in? He should have stayed inside. Should he tell the boy to go next door where there would at least be an adult? But the boy had chosen to come here. Perhaps he had seen Rohan watching him from the car and knew this was his house.

"We stay there." The boy pointed in the direction of the squatter camp. "I go to school there." He pointed in the direction of Mount View Primary. He was trying to reassure Rohan that it would be OK to open the gate. He was still in his school uniform but wore a pair of dirty-blue rubber sandals. His legs were as thin as sticks.

"Isn't there a doctor with your mother?" It was such a silly question that as soon as it was out, Rohan wished he could take it back. If they could afford a doctor, they wouldn't be squatters on a bare hillside. The boy shook his head vigorously. If he thought it was stupid, he didn't let it show on his troubled face.

"Wait there!" Rohan returned to the house. The button for the electric gate was inside the front door. The boy waited while the wrought-iron bars slowly rolled back.

"OK. Bring your buckets over here." Rohan pointed to the outside tap. The buckets clanked against each other as the boy jogged toward him.

"Thank you," he said quietly.

The unexpected softness in his voice had a strange effect on Rohan. It sounded so different from his own bossy tone. Suddenly he felt a little ashamed. This was the same boy whose wire cars he admired! If he were still at Mount View Primary they would probably be in the same class. They might even have been friends, and he would be learning how to make wire cars himself. Why had he spoken so arrogantly? It was really only a small favor that was being asked for. The water in the bucket gurgling and churning reminded Rohan of the water swirling beneath the Mozambican woman with her baby. *Her* rescuer had been taking a really big risk but hadn't looked big headed. He had just got on with the job.

When both buckets were full, the boy stooped to lift one on to his head. Rohan saw his face and neck muscles strain under the weight. How would he manage to keep it balanced and carry the other bucket too?

"Wait! I'll give you a hand." Rohan's offer was out before he had time to think it through properly. If the boy was surprised, he didn't show it. All his energy seemed to be focused on his task. Rohan dashed into the kitchen to grab the spare set of keys. Ma would be away for another hour at least. He would be back soon, and she need never know. It was only after the gate clicked behind them that Rohan remembered the neighbors. If anyone saw him, they were bound to ask Ma what he was doing with a boy from the squatter camp. He crossed the fingers of one hand.

At first Rohan said nothing. Sharing the weight of the bucket, he could feel the strain all the way up from his fingers to his left shoulder. When they reached the corner and set off down the hill, the bucket seemed to propel them forward. It was an effort to keep a steady pace. Rohan glanced at the container on the boy's head, marveling at how he kept it balanced. He caught the boy's eye.

"How do you do that? You haven't spilled a drop!"

The boy gave a glimmer of a smile.

"You learn."

Rohan liked the simple reply. He should ask the boy about the cars. This was his chance, before they turned into the noisy main road and reached the squatter camp.

"I've seen you with wire cars. Do you make them yourself?"

"Yes—and my brother."

"You make them together? Do you keep them all?"

"My brother—he sells them at the beach." The boy waved his free hand in the direction of the sea. "The tourists—they like them."

"Your cars are better than any I've seen in the shops! Do you get lots of money for them?"

"Mmhh!" The boy made a sound something between a laugh and a snort. Rohan realized that he had asked another brainless question. Would they be staying in a shack if they got lots of money? Rohan had often seen his own father bargaining to get something cheaper from a street hawker. He tried to cover his mistake.

"There's a shop in the mall where they sell wire

cars. They charge a lot and yours are a hundred times better!"

"We can't go there. The guards—they don't let us in."

Rohan knew the security guards at the entrance to the mall. Some of them even greeted his parents with a little salute. Rohan had seen poor children hanging around outside. They offered to push your trolley, to clean your car—anything for a few cents. Sometimes Ma gave an orange or an apple from her shopping bag to a child. Other times she would just say "No thank you" and wave a child away. Ma never gave money. She said they might spend it on drugs. Rohan had never thought what it would be like to be chased away. How did the guards decide who could enter? How could the boy and his brother go and show the lady in the African Crafts shop his cars if they weren't allowed in?

Rohan was quiet as they reached the main road and turned toward the squatter camp. The noise of vehicles roaring past was deafening. He never normally walked down here. Not by himself nor with anyone else. His family went everywhere by car. With all the locks down, of course. The only people who walked were poor people. His eyes were drawn to a group of young men walking toward them. They were still some distance away, but already Rohan began to feel uneasy. They were coming from the crossroads that his dad always approached on full alert. Rohan knew how his father jumped the red lights when the road was clear, especially at night. Everyone had heard stories of gangs who hijacked cars waiting for the lights to change.

The handle had begun to feel like it was cutting into his fingers. The boy must have sensed something because he signaled to Rohan to lower the bucket. For a few seconds they each stretched their fingers.

"It's too far? You want to go?" The boy was giving him a chance to change his mind. To leave and go back home. He had already helped carry the water more than half the way. He could make an excuse about the time. But the thought of running back to the house along the road on his own now worried him.

"No, it's fine. Let's go." Rohan heard a strange brightness in his own voice. He curled his fingers around the handle again.

As they drew nearer the men, Rohan felt their

gaze on him and suddenly his head was spinning with questions. Why on earth had he offered to help carry the water? What did he think he was doing coming down here? And he hadn't even yet entered the squatter camp itself!

"We go here." The boy's voice steadied him a little.

Rohan turned and stared up at his old ski slope. He felt the force of the young men's eyes on his back as he and the boy began to ascend the rough track. Someone behind called out something in Zulu and, without turning, the boy shouted back.

The words flew so quickly into one another that Rohan didn't pick up any even though he was learning Zulu in school. They must be talking about him, but he was too embarrassed—and frightened—to ask. He could feel his heart pumping faster and told himself it was because of the stiff climb. He needed to concentrate where he put each foot. The track was full of holes and small stones. A quick glance over his shoulder revealed that the young men had also entered the squatter camp but seemed to be heading for a shack with a roof covered in old tires on the lower slope. A couple of them were still watching. He must just look ahead and control his fear. As long as he was with the boy, he was safe, surely?

A bunch of small children appeared from nowhere, giggling and staring. He couldn't follow their chatter but heard the word *"iNdiya!"* The boy ignored them until a couple of children started darting back and forth in front of them, sweeping up the red dust with their feet.

"Hambani!" Rohan could hear the boy's irritation as he waved them away. But the darting and dancing continued just out of reach.

"Hambani-bo!" This time the boy's voice deepened to a threat, and the cluster of children pulled aside with one or two mischievous grins. Beads of sweat had begun trickling down the boy's face. With his own skin prickling with sticky heat, Rohan wondered at the wiry strength of the boy whose back, head, and bucket were still perfectly upright as they mounted the hill.

"It's that one—we stay there." The boy, at last, pointed to a structure of corrugated iron, wood, and black plastic a little further up. It was not far from the old fig trees. For a moment Rohan thought he would say something about his hideout which the first squatters had pulled down. But he stopped himself. Maybe the boy had even been one of them!

As they drew nearer, they heard a woman moaning and a couple of other women's voices that sounded as if they were comforting her. The boy lowered the bucket swiftly from his head and pushed aside a plywood sheet, the door to his home.

Rohan wasn't sure what to do. He knew he couldn't follow. The sounds from within scared him. The moans were rapid and painful. He remembered a picture in a book at school that had showed the head of a baby popping out between its mother's legs. There had been an argument among his friends about how such a big head could possibly fit through a small hole. From what he could hear now, it must hurt terribly.

Rohan folded his arms tightly, trying not to show how awkward he felt. The little children were still watching but keeping their distance. They could probably also hear the cries. It would be hard to keep anything private here. The only other people nearby were two gray-haired men sitting on boxes a little lower down the hill. One of them was bent over an old-fashioned sewing machine placed on a metal drum, a makeshift table. Normally Rohan would have been very curious to see what he was stitching, but now he was just grateful that both men were engrossed in talking and didn't seem interested in him.

He turned to look up the hill—toward his house and the others at the top protected by their walls with wires, spikes, and broken bottles. When he had hidden in his hideout down here, he had always loved the feeling of being safe yet almost in his own separate little country. But that had been a game and he could just hop over the wall to return to the other side. Surrounded now by homes made out of scraps and other people's left-overs, this place seemed a complete world away from the houses on the hill. In fact, how was he going to get home? If he didn't leave soon, Ma would be back before him. Would the boy at least take him part of the way through the squatter camp? He needed him to come outside so that he could ask him.

"What do you want here?"

Rohan spun around. A man with half-closed eyes and his head tilted to one side stood with his hands on his hips, surveying Rohan from head to foot. His gaze lingered for a moment on Rohan's watch.

"I . . . I brought water with . . . with . . ." Rohan stammered. He hadn't asked the boy his name! Panic-stricken, he pointed to the door of the shack. The man stepped forward, and Rohan stumbled back against the wall of corrugated iron. The clattering brought the boy to the door. The man immediately switched into loud, fast Zulu. The boy spoke quietly at first, but when the man's voice didn't calm down, the boy's began to rise too. Even when he pointed to the bucket and Rohan, the man's face remained scornful. Rohan was fully expecting to be grabbed when a sharp baby's cry interrupted the argument. The boy's face lit up, and the man suddenly fell silent. Rohan's heart thumped wildly as the man's eyes mocked him before he turned and walked away.

Rohan folded his arms tightly, trying not to shake. Before he could say anything, a lady appeared behind the boy, placing a hand on his shoulder.

"You have a little sister!" She smiled at the boy and then at Rohan. She looked friendly but tired. Her cheeks shone as if she too had been perspiring. It was obviously hard work helping to deliver a baby.

"Tell your mother thank you for the water. You really helped us today."

Rohan managed to smile back.

"It's OK." His voice came out strangely small.

"Solani will take you back now—before it gets dark."

Rohan felt a weight lifting. He did not need to ask.

The sun was getting lower and made long rodlike shadows leap beside them as they scrambled down the slope. Knowing the boy's name made Rohan feel a little easier, and he wondered why he hadn't asked him earlier. He told Solani his own, and the next thing he was telling him about riding on garbage can lids down the ski slope. Solani grinned.

"It's good! But this place—it's a road now. We can't do it. The people will be angry if we knock someone down."

Rohan understood that. But what he didn't understand was why the man with scornful eyes had been so angry with him. And why had those other young men looked at him so suspiciously? He decided to ask Solani.

"They don't know you. Sometimes people come

and attack us. So if a stranger comes, they must always check first."

When they reached the road, neither spoke. The hometime traffic would have drowned their voices anyway. Rohan thought about what Solani had said about him being a stranger. Surely they knew that he was from one of the houses on top of the hill. The houses that also did not welcome strangers. Like the squatters.

They parted at the top of the hill. Rohan was anxious to reach the house before his mother returned, and Solani was eager to see his baby sister. Opening the electronic gates, Rohan was relieved that his mother's car was neither in the yard nor the garage. He dashed upstairs to his room and peered out of the window over to the squatter camp. The evening was falling very rapidly. His mother would be home any minute—and his dad. Neither liked to drive in the dark if they could help it.

Rohan fixed his eyes on the deep crimson scar, hoping to see Solani climbing the slope. How strange to think that he had been there himself less than half an hour ago. In that other world. Yes! There was Solani! A tiny, wiry figure bounding up the hill. Not hampered this time with a container of water on his head. Rohan watched Solani weave through other figures traveling more slowly until three quarters of the way up the hill, he darted off and disappeared into the darkening shadow that was his home.

Rohan surprised his parents by joining them for the eight o'clock news. The story about the rescue of mother and baby from the floods in Mozambique was repeated.

"Sophia Pedro and her baby daughter Rositha were among the lucky few. Many thousands of Mozambicans are still waiting to be lifted to safety. . . ."

This time the reporter added their names. Rohan observed the mother more closely. Had she also cried and moaned like Solani's mother? With the roaring waters underneath, how many people had heard her?

"It's nice to see these South African soldiers doing some good," said Ma when the news was finished.

Rohan wished he could say what he too had done that afternoon. But he feared the storm that it would let loose and went upstairs to his bedroom. Before slipping between his sheets, he peered out once again through the bars at the hill swallowed up by the night. He thought he saw a light still flickering in Solani's home and wondered how many people were tucked inside the sheets of iron, plastic, and wood. He prayed that Cyclone Gloria would keep well away.

Next morning, the glint of metal beside the gate caught his eye from the front door. His dad was reversing the car out of the garage. Rohan ran across the drive. There, just inside the gate, was a wire car. A small, perfect Merc! Who could it be from, except Solani? He must have slipped it through the bars of the gate in the early morning. Quickly Rohan pushed it behind a cluster of scarlet gladioli. If his parents saw it, they would want to know from where it had come. They would discover he had gone out of bounds. . . . Well, so had Solani! Each of them had taken a risk. He needed time to think. In the meantime, the car would have to be his secret. Their secret. His and Solani's.

TIMELINE ACROSS APARTHEID

1948   *The Dare*

Afrikaner Nationalists take over the government. They promise to tighten racism through apartheid laws. Earlier whites-only governments (supported mainly by English speakers) have already passed many laws that discriminate against black South Africans. The African National Congress has protested peacefully for years.

1949   *The Noose*

Prohibition of Mixed Marriages Act. Black and white South Africans are forbidden to marry.

1950   *The Noose*

Population Registration Act. Everyone must be classified according to a so-called "racial group:" "White"; "Colored"; "Indian"; "Native" or "Bantu," i.e. Black African. The definitions are scientific nonsense, but they become law. Classification affects everything about a person's life. Some families are split when children of mixed heritage are classified differently because of differences in the shade of their skin or curliness of their hair.

The Noose

The Group Areas Act. People are forced to live in separate areas according to the "racial group" in which they have been put.

One Day, Lily, One Day

The Suppression of Communism Act. People are listed as "communists" if they actively fight against apartheid. They can be banned from meeting other people, confined to a particular area, or banished to a faraway place.

1952   *One Day, Lily, One Day*

The Abolition of Passes Act. All Africans are forced to carry a single passbook that controls where they can live and work.

1953   *The Typewriter; The Playground*

The Bantu Education Act. African children are given a different syllabus that prepares them only for low-grade work.

The Noose; One Day, Lily, One Day
The Separate Amenities Act. Black and white people
are forbidden to use the same parks, beaches,
buses, trains, sports grounds, cinemas, etc. A black
nursemaid may go on a "white" beach if she is
looking after a white child but cannot go into the
water.

1955   *One Day, Lily, One Day*
At the Congress of the People, 3,000 delegates
from across the country and of all backgrounds
meet on open ground near Johannesburg. They
declare the Freedom Charter. It includes the words
"South Africa belongs to all who live in it, black
and white. . . ."

1956   *One Day, Lily, One Day*
One hundred and fifty-six South Africans of all
backgrounds are arrested and charged with trea-
son. Some remain on trial until 1961, when they
are found not guilty.

1960   *One Day, Lily, One Day*
Police open fire at Africans marching peacefully to
Sharpeville Police Station without their passbooks.

They intend to be arrested as a protest. Instead, over two hundred are injured and sixty-nine killed, including children. A State of Emergency is declared. The African National Congress and the Pan-Africanist Congress are banned and many thousands are arrested.

1961–4   *The Gun*

Nelson Mandela and others go "underground." The ANC forms *Umkhonto we Sizwe (MK)* or Spear of the Nation to train soldiers and fight an "underground" war. They begin with bombing electricity pylons and buildings. But in 1963, Nelson Mandela and eight others, including two white comrades, are put on trial and face the death sentence. Eight are sentenced to life imprisonment. Many others are arrested, kept in jail without trial, tortured, sentenced to long terms in jail. Some are sentenced to death.

1976   *The Typewriter*

Thousands of black secondary school students in Soweto protest when the government says half their lessons will, from now on, be taught in Afrikaans. Police open fire, killing children. Anger explodes across the country. Hundreds of young people are killed in demonstrations and many more thousands are thrown into jail. Many young people escape from the country, some to train with MK..

1985–6   *The Gun*
The government calls another State of Emergency. Despite its harsh laws, the struggle against apartheid has still continued within the country and through freedom fighters coming across the borders.

1990   *The Playground*
Nelson Mandela is released from jail to help negotiate a new system of government. The world watches on television as he walks out of prison after twenty-seven years in jail.

1994   *The Playground*
South Africa holds its first free, democratic elections. The African National Congress forms the government, and Nelson Mandela is elected President. Apartheid laws are cancelled but work now has to begin to try and repair the terrible damage.

1995   *The Playground*

At the beginning of the New Year, for the first time, schools must open their doors to all children. Some white parents and teachers still want to resist.

2000   *Out of Bounds*

The new century begins with floods that devastate parts of southern Africa, especially Mozambique. The South African army, which in the past has dropped bombs on Mozambique, helps in the rescue of flood victims.

OUT OF
BOUNDS

A Q&A with Beverley Naidoo

My Banned Book

An Excerpt from Beverley's Novel
Burn My Heart

A Q&A with Beverley Naidoo

You write mostly novels. What inspired you to make a collection of short stories?

Short stories are a challenge to write because they have to be so compact. I once heard Nadine Gordimer, the South African Nobel Laureate, say that the short story has to be like an egg. Every part has to connect to every other part. "The Dare," "The Typewriter," "The Gun," and "The Playground" were originally published in different collections in the United Kingdom. It occurred to me that each was set in a different decade in South Africa and that the characters and their stories said something about "being at that point in time." If each set of characters could step in front of a mirror, the wider picture behind them would reflect the changing history. All I had to do was fill in the gaps and I would have a collection of seven stories set in seven decades. So, in 2000, I decided to write stories for the 1950s, 1960s, and the year 2000.

Did writing stories that had to be set in particular decades change the writing process?

I started by considering what were really important events before I began to think about my characters. The classification of everyone in the country into one of four so-called "racial groups" was something terrible and fundamental in the 1950s. That led me to think about a child who experiences the shock of discovering what classification means to him and his family. For the 1960s, I knew that my story had to involve the massacre at Sharpeville because that changed the course of history in South Africa. I decided to explore what the event might mean to a white child whose background was different from mine and that of most other white children. Lily's parents completely reject apartheid. They are brave and teach Lily important values of equality, justice, and respect. But this means that Lily finds herself the odd one out in her whites-only school. Like every child, Lily wants friendship, and her inner conflict gives a strong dynamic that leads into the bigger story.

How did you create a story for the year 2000 when the decade was only beginning?

I thought about the millennium and how we were moving from one century to another. Extraordinary floods hit the East African coast as the new century began, and I recalled the amazing image on television of a Mozambican mother who gave birth to her baby in a tree. It was such a symbol of resilience, courage, and hope in the midst of disaster. Already by 2000, people were saying that our world has become so unstable that the twenty-first century will be the "century of refugees." I also wanted to explore the vast, dangerous divide between the "haves" and "have nots." The divide lives on after the ending of apartheid and is also global. That led me to think about Rohan in his comfortable house at the top of the hill and Solani in his rickety, fragile home on the slope below. I called the story "Out of Bounds" because each boy crosses a boundary. It is not just a physical boundary, but each takes a vital step forward in crossing boundaries of the mind and, I believe, of the heart.

Are any of the stories based on you or your personal experiences?

Like other fiction writers, I often delve deep into myself and my imagination as I try to make sense of things that have intrigued, puzzled, or troubled me. Nicky's parents in "The Dare" take her to a guest farm under a mountain in the Magaliesberg, which is where my parents used to take my brother and me. We were "townies," and I remember wanting to be accepted by the family of white children who lived on the farm and who were a lot tougher than I was. There are details from real life in the story, including the one-legged chameleon and the doll Margaret, which I still have! However, the events that take place are fiction, although, at a deep level, I was exploring the idea of how easily we become implicated in an immoral system.

Most of the stories contain things remembered

and transformed. In "One Day, Lily, One Day," Lily's teachers run in panic to shut the school gates because of a false rumor. That happened in my school for white girls on March 21, 1960, the day of the Sharpeville massacre. In "The Typewriter," Khulu bravely tries to hide the typewriter in one of the garages like those at the back of the apartment block where I grew up. The idea of a story about a typewriter used for resistance work came from the typewriter that my brother hid behind the kitchen cupboard in the apartment that I rented after leaving home. Very fortunately, the security police who raided my apartment never found it.

You have adapted "The Playground" into a stage play. What was that like?

I transformed rather than adapted it! I had to pull apart my very compact short story and dig up every tension within it. I added a third act so I could explore Rosa and Hennie when they were sixteen. I learned much more about my characters, especially through workshops with actors and my director, Olusola Oyeleye. We went out to South Africa as part of the research and development process. I wove traditional songs throughout my script, as music is part of life in South Africa and conveys emotion so powerfully. *The Playground* premiered at the Polka Theatre in London in 2004 and was a *Time Out* Critics' Choice Pick of the Year.

My Banned Book

My first children's book, *Journey to Jo'burg*, was published in the UK in March 1985. I sent two copies to South Africa for my nephews and nieces but the books never arrived. Instead, my sister-in-law received a nasty letter telling her that *Journey to Jo'burg* had been banned and "seized." The apartheid government had stolen my books! They banned the book as soon as they realized that half its royalties were going to a forbidden organization, the British Defense and Aid Fund for Southern Africa. This fund helped political prisoners and their families—people like Nelson Mandela and so many others who struggled against apartheid and whose families were left without breadwinners. But I was surprised at how quickly the authorities had outlawed *Journey to Jo'burg*. I was also angry and upset. How ridiculous that they would threaten to arrest someone for wanting to read a story!

I wrote "They Tried to Lock Up Freedom" nearly twenty years later, after the course of history was changed in my birth country. But my poem is not just about South Africa. Wherever we are faced with bullies and violence, it is about the truth in the old saying "The pen is mightier than the sword." Or, as a ten year old once told me, "The sword has no imagination. It can only kill. The pen has imagination."

They Tried To Lock Up Freedom

They seized the book
Ripped out its spine
Flung it in the fire

    Pages fluttered through smoke

They grabbed the pages
Scratched out lines
Crushed them in their fists

    Words squeezed through knuckles

They twisted the words
Tore out sound
Swallowed them in their silence

    The heart of the book cried out
      The pages grew wings
        The words breathed Freedom

Beverley Naidoo

**DOEANE EN AKSYNS
CUSTOMS AND EXCISE**

DIE KONTROLEUR VAN DOEANE EN AKSYNS
THE CONTROLLER OF CUSTOMS AND EXCISE

PRIVATE BAG X54305

Republiek
van
Suid-Afrika

Republic
of
South Africa

DURBAN   4000

☎ 378511   Uitbreiding
Extension 234

Navrae
Enquiries   Mr Roth

☏ "DOEAKS"

My verwysing
My reference   9/5/6/2/ล

Datum
Date   198 -05- 2 2

Mrs S. Naidoo
Farm Taurus
P.O. Box 24
KEARSNEY
4453

Madam

UNDESIRABLE PUBLICATION : A JOURNEY TO JO'BURG –
2 COPIES.

The abovementioned literature addressed to you ex UK has been ruled by the
Directorate of Publications to be undesirable and importation is prohibited vide
Section 113(1)(f) of the Customs and Excise Act No. 91 of 1964.

The books are therefore seized in terms of Sections 87, 88 and 89 of the Customs
Act and a transcript is attached for your information.

Yours faithfully

CONTROLLER OF CUSTOMS AND EXCISE

A STORM OUTSIDE

Mathew curled up under his crisp cotton sheet, listening to the rain drumming on the tin roof. It was a stroke of luck. By the time Father inspected around the fence in the morning light, his and Mugo's tracks on the other side would be washed away. Father need never know of their expedition. Usually the sound of rain on the tin induced Mathew into sleep. He enjoyed feeling wrapped up securely from the elements outside. But after the telephone call from Major Smithers, he didn't feel safe at all.

He was used to hearing grown-ups talk about the Mau Mau, especially at the club. But whenever he asked where an incident had happened, he was told "*Fortunately, not here.*" It had always been somewhere else . . . like Nairobi, which they seldom visited, or Naivasha or some other place in the Rift Valley on the other side of the Aberdare Mountains.

Tonight, however, Mathew lay in bed imagining that people might actually be prowling around their farm. What a fool he had been! What if the fence had been cut by a Mau Mau gang and they had met them in the bush? That would have been even more terrifying than their encounter with One-Tusk . . . and Mugo wouldn't have been able to protect him, a white settler boy.

The rain beat down harder now, rattling the roof, as thunder rumbled in the distance. When Mathew was younger, he had often run into the stables to get out of a thunderstorm. He and Kamau would watch the heavens open, drenching the garden and the bush beyond. In Kamau's stories, Ngai the Creator rolled out thunder from the top of his mountain when he was angered. There was one story in which Elephant helped Hare to cross a river. Hare offered to hold Elephant's jar of honey while sitting on his back. By the time they reached the other side, the jar was empty. Hare was laughing but Elephant was furious at Hare's deceit and vowed revenge. Mathew could hear Kamau ending the story as if he had made it specially for him, the little master: "*You see, bwana kidogo, one day Ngai will help Elephant. That day Hare will be very sorry. Bwana kidogo, you must know that Ngai sees everything."* Mathew coiled in his head like a snail as he remembered how it had felt to be at the mercy of One-Tusk and his anger. As the lightning cracked, splitting the night sky, he pulled his pillow over his head.

STRANGERS

Mugo woke in the middle of the night. The first thing he heard was rain rushing to the earth. He urgently needed to pee but waited to let his eyes adjust to the gloom so he wouldn't trip over his brother and sister sleeping on the floor beside him. As he tiptoed across the room, a drop of water splashed his forehead. The thatch was leaking again. He had helped Baba patch it up in the last rainy season. He skirted past the bed where Baba was snoring. His father slept lightly and Mugo hoped the rain would cover the sound of him tugging the metal bolt on the door. Then he opened the creaking wood just enough to squeeze out. He eased it shut behind him.

Sheets of water pitched down from the edge of the thatch. The rain was driving a stream across the compound and he decided against trying to reach the toilet area. Instead, hugging the wall, he hurried to the back of the house to relieve himself there. He took his time, enjoying the freshness of the air and the damp earth. The rain was a blessing. With luck it would help everyone forget the incident of the fence.

He was feeling his way back when he realized that he was not alone in the compound. He pressed his back against the wall, his heart thumping. Three shadows were slicing through the torrential rain, aiming for the room where his parents were sleeping. They were almost close enough to touch with a long stick! The one in front was bent double, carrying something. A gun? The door was unbolted and they could go straight in! There was no chance of Mugo getting back inside in time to lock it.

His instinct told him to hide. Could he conceal himself between the maize stalks in the shamba? But he needed to know what was happening. Diving through the rain, he reached the entrance to the shamba and, trembling, felt his way along its thorny hedge until he thought he was in line with the front of the house. He scratched his fingers trying to feel for an opening through which he could peer. The downpour was easing slightly and he could just make out a shape standing outside like a guard. Then Baba's and Mami's shapes came stumbling through the door. They were probably

still half asleep. There was no screaming or shouting but Mami huddled close to his father. Where
were his little brother and sister? Had his parents
been forced out of bed so quietly that the little
ones were still sleeping?

More shadows emerged and there was talking.
Mugo strained to hear. One of the strangers was
much shorter than the others and his high-pitched
voice carried through the rain.

"Where is the kitchen toto?"

". . . not here . . . sometimes he sleeps there . . .
kitchen . . . Mzungu keeps him late . . ." Baba's
bass voice was more difficult to follow but Mugo
also saw him wave his arm towards the bwana's
house.

"If you lie, you will pay." The words flew sharp
as arrows.

Mugo's mouth felt dry. How did these young
men know about him? If they had an informant,
they would soon know Baba was lying. He had only
once slept in the shed by the kitchen.

"Why should I lie?" Baba sounded composed.
"Are we not coming with you without trouble?"

"Must I look, captain?" The shape of the guard
stepped away from the door.

"Hapana. No, we go." It was the same rapid, higher voice that had asked about the kitchen toto. He was the one with the gun and clearly the leader. Mugo was surprised how short he was, probably not much taller than himself. Mugo made out a peaked cap but could see nothing of the face underneath.

With Mami and Baba between them, the young men headed briskly toward the row of banana trees that separated Mugo's compound from Mzee Josiah's. Mugo was torn. Shouldn't he go back to his brother and sister? That's what his parents would want him to do. But he also had to know where the strangers were taking them! He would lose them in the rain-filled night if he didn't follow instantly.

The shamba extended almost to the banana trees but the thorn hedge was so thickly planted that it would be difficult to get out at that end. He was obliged to hurry back to the shamba's entrance and, by the time he was running softly on the other side, he had lost the figures in the thick wet darkness. Mugo imagined, however, that they might be heading for Mzee Josiah's door. In daylight you could see it from the banana trees, but as he emerged through the web of dripping leaves, he realized he would have to sneak up closer to see anything.

Mzee Josiah and his wife lived on their own. Their children were all grown up, working in Nairobi and Nyeri as clerks and teachers, for more money than their parents could ever earn. Halfway between the banana trees and the house was a fat mango tree. Mzee Josiah claimed his mangoes were juicier than any in the memsahib's orchard and that his cook's nose could sniff out any young thieves. When ripe, the sweet golden finger-licking smell of the fruit was a great temptation. Occasionally, made bold by friends, Mugo risked capturing a couple of mangoes. With his blood pulsing just as strongly now, he trod softly toward the tree. Tonight the rain was his friend, covering his sounds! But as he slid between the mesh of mango branches and leaves, he felt a thousand fingers circling his neck. Seconds later, he heard a shout, a scream, then scuffling and muffled shrieks. Even the gun hadn't made Mzee Josiah and Mama Mercy come as quietly as Baba and Mami.

"Stop their mouths!" It was the captain again. "Haraka! Hurry! These ones will make us late!"

Late for what? No one said it, but it was understood. Mugo's hammering heart knew . . . just as it knew why they had asked for him too.